"Taste," she commanded, pushing the glass wine of toward him.

Tension pulled taut in Wyatt's gut. He picked up the glass.

"Bouquet?" she asked bluntly.

Okay, if that was the way it was going to be, he could handle a little rough and tumble. He nailed her with his gaze and they stepped into a silent, motionless waltz.

"Supple," Wyatt replied.

"What else?" Her pupils narrowed.

"Complex."

"And," she nudged.

He half expected her to poke him with one of those long, slender fingers. *Good God, she's magnificent.*

"Well?" She was a pushy one.

"Surprising," Wyatt said, but he was not speaking of the wine.

"Impertinent," she said.

"The wine?"

"You."

"Now who's being impertinent?"

Her cheeks reddened with effrontery.

Finally. He'd rattled her. Setting his glass on the table, he stalked toward her. Wine wouldn't be the only thing he'd be tasting this evening.

Dear Reader,

A couple of years ago I made my first trip to Napa Valley and I was immediately captivated by the craft of winemaking. It's such a sexy, romantic endeavor, more art than science, although modern technology has made the production of high-quality wines more consistent. At its heart, the growing and nurturing of grapes is a true labor of love.

But it's not just winemaking that's so romantic. It's the lush rolling hills and the misty foggy mornings. The soft silence combined with the profound earthiness of the land; the oaken smell of aging barrels, the warmth of the noonday sun burning off the dew, the cozy darkness of wine cellars. Vineyards are fertile with life. Throw in a legend about lovers in such an idyllic place and you have the makings of a red-hot story.

So come along on the journey as corporate raider Wyatt DeSalme plays undercover spy at Bella Notte vineyards, only to discover that scientist Kiara Romano is going to change him in ways that this die-hard charmer never believed possible.

I hope you enjoy Wyatt and Kiara's story, and do check out the other great books on the shelf this month from Harlequin Blaze! Ciao for now.

Happy reading,

Lori Wilde

Lori Wilde

INTOXICATING

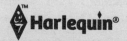

TORONTO NEW YORK LONDON
AMSTERDAM PARIS SYDNEY HAMBURG
STOCKHOLM ATHENS TOKYO MILAN MADRID
PRAGUE WARSAW BUDAPEST AUCKLAND

Recycling programs
for this product may
not exist in your area.

ISBN-13: 978-0-373-79652-6

INTOXICATING

www.Harlequin.com

Printed in U.S.A.

ABOUT THE AUTHOR

Lori Wilde is the author of forty books. She's been nominated for a RITA® Award and four *RT Book Reviews* Reviewers' Choice Awards. Her books have been excerpted in *Cosmopolitan, Redbook* and *Quick & Simple*. Lori teaches writing online through Ed2go. She's also an RN trained in forensics, and she volunteers at a women's shelter. Visit her website at www.loriwilde.com.

Books by Lori Wilde

To Michael Lee West,
who showed me the magic of list-making.

1

Amabile: *In Italian* loveable.
Used to indicate a sweet wine.

AT DAWN ON the first day of June, Wyatt DeSalme stood on the bow of the ferry watching the mist-shrouded island that lay just off the coast of northern California slide into view.

The churning engines vibrated up through the deck floor and he tasted salty sea air. Seagulls chattered like gossiping biddies and the excited voices of the young men and women surrounding him, nursing their gourmet coffees and noshing on free pastries, grew in tone and tempo as the mist parted.

Suddenly, the jagged, double-barrelled bluff known as Twin Hearts jutted straight up from the middle of the island, glistening in the jubilant glow of morning light.

This was it. His destination.

The strangest feeling passed over him, a feeling that said, *If you do this, you'll never be the same.*

An uneasy knot settled in the pit of his stomach.

I don't wanna go.

How come? Normally, he loved role-playing. Secret agent man had been his favorite game as a kid, not cowboys and Indians like this brothers. Why the sudden impulse to stay rooted on the boat while everyone else disembarked?

What's the matter? Chicken?

The taunt came from the back of his mind, but it was the voice of his oldest brother, Scott, issuing the chanting dare from childhood along with an excess of poultry noises; a dare Wyatt had never been able to resist. It was why he'd broken a collarbone climbing a quince tree when he was ten, and why he'd fallen through the ice on a barely frozen pond when they'd visited their maternal grandparents in Kansas one Christmas. The taunts, dares, bets and challenges had gone a long way toward forming his character. Always eager to prove himself to his older brothers, he had turned into a bold adventurer. Now here he was at thirty-one still trying to win their approval.

As a disguise, he wore dark-framed, non-prescription lenses and two days' growth of prickly beard. Over the past few months he'd let his hair grow out, getting ready for this covert game, and it curled in waves to his collar. He hadn't worn his hair this long since college and an errant strand kept flopping across his brow whenever he tilted his head forward.

He had on blue jeans with a hole in one knee, a gray knit cap and a gray hooded sweatshirt emblazoned with the Berkeley University logo, a school he had not attended, but wished he had. He'd gone instead to Princeton, as was family tradition, and had dropped out in his sophomore year. His sneakers—purchased at a thrift shop—boasted broken shoelaces and thin treads. His watch, also from the thrift store, was a cheap drugstore brand. He'd left the Rolex at his condo in Athens. No belt. No socks.

His goal? Downplay his looks. Make himself as nondescript as possible. Fit in with the opposite of his customary behavior. Normally, Wyatt adored wearing a tux to high-society parties, driving his Lamborghini on the autobahn, gambling in Monte Carlo and generally being the center of attention.

The dodge seemed to be working. He'd been on the boat for over an hour and not a single one of the hot coeds on board had shot him a second glance. Which was both reassuring and a bit of an ego-crusher.

"So," said one of those gorgeous coeds to another as the engines stopped churning and the ferry glided toward the dock. "Do you think the legend of Idyll Island is true?"

Wyatt, eager to eavesdrop on their conversation, moved closer to the two young women who stood near the railing watching the ferry workers prep for landing. A good corporate spy kept his eyes and ears open.

"What's that?" asked the second girl. The petite brunette looked barely legal, but he'd heard her say earlier that she was as an intern at Belle Notte Vineyards, so she had to be at least twenty-one. Still, she could pass for a high-school student.

You're just getting old.

He quickly batted away that thought. He was thirty-one, in the prime of life, at the top of his game.

"Oh, you haven't heard? It's amazing. So romantic." The first girl, a blonde with a pert ski-slope of a nose, dramatically clutched both hands to her heart. "Here's how the story goes. Way back, a long, long time ago, when the founder of Bella Notte, Giovanni Romano, was our age, he fell in love with a girl from the mainland. One night in June, Giovanni took the first bottle of wine produced from his vineyard, along with his sweetheart, Maria, up to the top of Twin Hearts." The blonde paused and gestured at the towering bluffs.

"Did they do it up there?" The brunette giggled.

Wyatt rolled his eyes, but sidled closer.

"I'm sure." The blonde grinned slyly. "They shared the wine underneath the full moon, and then Giovanni asked Maria to marry him. She said yes. They were married in the vineyard the following June and lived happily ever after for sixty-four years."

"Aww, that's so sweet."

"Giovanni and Maria's three sons did the same thing with their girlfriends. And then *their* sons did too. No one in the Romano family has ever been divorced. Nor has anyone who has ever shared a bottle of wine with their true love on Twin Hearts during a full moon in June."

"No one?"

The blonde shook her head. "No one."

"Wow," said the brunette. "Those are some crazy odds."

What a load of bull, Wyatt thought, but in spite of himself, he was charmed by the legend. He had to admit that the Romanos sure knew how to stir up a myth for publicity and he wondered how much of the boutique vineyard's success was tied into that farfetched story.

"Well, I'm not here for romance," the blonde said. "I'm here to learn winemaking from the best."

"Couldn't get an internship at DeSalme Vineyards, huh?"

"No," the blonde admitted sheepishly. "But this is better."

"How do you figure?"

"Belle Notte's a small winery, run by a woman."

"And there *is* that legend."

"I told you I'm not interested in romance. Now hooking up with a hot guy… She cast a sidelong glance at the deckhands docking the boat. "Absolutely. I'm just not in the market for happily ever after."

Me neither.

Wyatt slid an appraising glance over the blonde. Apart from her youthfuness, she was what his brothers would refer to as one of "Wyatt's Lamborghini women"—fast, sleek and expensive to maintain. She possessed a smoking body, expensive haircut and designer clothes. Too bad he couldn't afford the distraction.

"Not even if…you know…like you met somebody special, like, The One?" the brunette asked.

The blonde tossed her head. "I'm not ruling anything out, but yeah, I'm not interested in long-term. Not for years and years and years. I want to be like Kiara Romano, running my own winery by the time I'm thirty. You can't achieve something like that if you let your heart rule your head."

"It also helps to inherit a winery."

"There is that."

"Or marry into one."

The blonde sniffed. "I want to be the one in the driver's seat."

"It's not always pleasant behind the wheel. I heard Kiara never dates." The brunette lowered her voice and said something he couldn't hear.

Wyatt cocked his head, straining to listen, but it was too late. The women were moving away from him, heading to where everyone else was disembarking and climbing into the waiting vans whose doors wore mural wraps of Bella Notte Vineyards.

At this hour of the morning it seemed almost everyone on the ferry was a new intern headed for Bella Notte. Wyatt found himself in the same van with the chatty coeds. They ended up introducing themselves. The blonde's name was Lauren; the brunette's Bernadette.

As the caravan of four vehicles, each carrying six interns, drove up the hillside, the mist seemed to move with them, rolling away from the coast, rising up to cloak Twin Hearts. The landscape was arid earth on one side of the bluff, verdant valleys dotted with vineyards on the other. Idyll had the same grape-friendly climate as the Napa Valley region, the same easygoing feel.

The entrance to Bella Notte was as quaint as everything else on Idyll. A vine-covered stone wall flanked buildings reminiscent of Tuscan wineries. Beyond the buildings stretched rows of perfectly-manicured grapes. Wyatt had grown up in vineyards and honestly, they'd never interested him—too much hard work to be sure— but now, looking at this place, breathing in the scent of the rich loamy soil, his chest tightened and he felt oddly inspired.

His brothers would get a good laugh out of that. Why should he feel inspired by this tiny winery, while the big, sprawling corporate affair that was DeSalme Vineyards left him cold?

That reminded him of why he was here. To find out exactly what Belle Notte was doing that had caused this tiny boutique winery to take a surprising bite out of

DeSalme's market share. Their wines were supremely good. What were they doing differently? His brothers had paid to have the wine analyzed, but they'd been unable to detect why it was so special. They needed a corporate spy on the inside and he was it.

A tall, dark-haired man met the group and ushered them into one of the stone buildings. He moved with a dreamy, loose-limbed stride, as if walking on a bank of clouds. He wore his hair long, swept off his forehead and tied back with a leather strap. He had a cluster of purple grapes tattooed on his right forearm and he wore a shirt made from hemp. The artsy look made Wyatt think of the skinny, ponytailed guy on the cover of the Fleetwood Mac *Rumours* album.

A raven-haired woman, wearing a gauzy blue dress, ambled across the yard to join them. She nestled against the tall man and turned her face up to receive a long, soulful kiss from him. With genuine affection, the man patted her butt, and then gently tugged her along beside him.

It was cool inside and minimally furnished with a large, sturdy wooden table and a long row of matching chairs. It was obviously a tasting room set up for the tourists who paid extra for lessons on wine- and food-pairing.

The place smelled of grapes: sweet and robust and intoxicating. It was a familiar scent that never quite left Wyatt's nostrils, no matter where in the world he sailed his yacht. But here in this austere room, he could not shake the aroma of home.

The back door opened, revealing a long corridor paneled in rich mahogany. Everyone turned in unison.

A woman about his own age entered the room,

dressed in a style that Wyatt could only describe as "you're not getting a gander at the goods, smart guy." She wore round wire-framed granny glasses, a shapeless, floral dress that he associated with women over sixty and a burgundy-and-green Bella Notte chef's apron.

The dress hem hit her at mid-calf and her feet were shod in battered tan hiking boots with thick rubber soles. A pair of simple gold studs lay nestled in her earlobes and her complexion was as sunkissed as field grapes and completely without the artifice of makeup. She'd pulled her dark auburn hair back in a haphazard ponytail, escaping strands poking out in every direction.

For some weird reason, the song, "Every Which Way but Loose" popped into his mind.

She raised her head and her stunning green eyes slammed into his and his heart just...*stumbled.*

A sudden memory flashed.

He was a child running through the grapevines, playing tag with his brothers and cousins during some outdoor event hosted by his family, the air rife with the smell of barbecue. He couldn't have been more than four or five. He'd reached the end of the row and then...*boom.*

Out of nowhere a little auburn-haired, green-eyed girl appeared. Momentum had been against him and he'd knocked her flat on the ground. She'd lain there staring at him in exactly the same way this woman was staring at him now.

As if he was an ugly bug in her breakfast cereal.

She knows!

Uncustomary panic seized him. This was more than

a game, he realized suddenly. There was more than his pride at stake. He'd told his brothers he could do this and Wyatt hated to fail. Besides, he was ready for more responsibility. He was tired of being the butt of his older brothers' jokes. He deserved to be a real part of the DeSalme legacy. If he could deliver Bella Notte's secret, it would prove him worthy and they'd have to stop dismissing him as just their playboy kid brother.

To wriggle out of her glower, he did what he always did when he aimed to charm women. He grinned and winked wolfishly.

Hey, stupid, you're not supposed to call attention to yourself.

The ploy worked. She glanced away quickly, pulled a corkscrew from her apron pocket and reached for a bottle of wine resting on the sideboard.

"Have a seat." The tall man waved a hand at the twenty-four empty chairs.

Everyone sat.

The man grabbed for glasses hanging from the rack suspended over the table and started passing them out. Three glasses apiece—a wide-bodied one for the reds, more elongated for the whites, narrow flutes for the dessert wines.

The auburn-haired woman swiftly opened various bottles of wines. Next, she was slipping between the interns, tipping an ounce of each kind of wine into the waiting glasses in movements as choreographed as a dance. She'd done this many, many times before.

"I'm Maurice Romano," the man said and moved to slide his hand around the black-haired woman's waist. "This is my wife, Trudy. Besides looking after our four children, she runs the gift shop and she is in charge of guest services."

Trudy Romano smiled. "Welcome, welcome. We want you to all feel part of the family."

The door opened and four kids trouped in. Two boys and two girls.

"This is Mia," Trudy said, putting her hands on the shoulders of the oldest girl. "She's thirteen."

Dark-haired Mia rolled her eyes. "Mom, they don't care."

Her mother ignored her. "This is Samuel. He's ten."

Samuel wore a Yankees baseball cap. He doffed it, bowed and grinned.

"Stop showing off." Mia thumped her brother.

"Keep your hands to yourself."

"Children, children," Trudy chided. "This is Elliott and he's seven."

Elliott beamed, showing two missing front teeth.

"This is Juliet. She's six."

Bashful Juliet turned and buried her face in her mother's skirt.

"I have to take them to school now, but we wanted to be here to greet you." Then waving, Trudy herded her brood out the door.

"And this," Maurice said, indicating the other woman, "is my cousin Kiara. Our great-grandparents started Bella Notte Vineyards in 1934 and it's been in our family ever since."

So this was the fabled Kiara Romano, supposedly so gifted she'd brought the struggling vineyard from the brink of bankruptcy to become one of the most promising boutique wineries in California. Wyatt straight-

ened in his chair. He certainly wouldn't have guessed
that from looking at her.

She stood directly across the table from him, pouring a chilled white wine for Lauren, the blonde from
the ferry. Kiara lifted her chin and their gazes met a
second time. Her mouth pressed into a tight thin line
and her emerald eyes narrowed.

What was this? Had she taken an instant dislike to
him? That was strange. Most women liked him. That
is, until they figured out he wasn't the kind of man who
believed in strings.

Kiara moved around the table, coming closer.

Wyatt's body tensed. He didn't hear what Maurice
was saying because all his focus was concentrated on
the woman pouring the wine.

She affected him on a visceral level, but he couldn't
say why. Maybe it was the graceful way she moved
even in those heavy boots. Maybe it was the appealing
contrast between her delicate bone structure and her
all-business, no-nonsense attitude. Maybe it was just
the romantic setting.

But if it was Bella Notte that had captured his imagination, then why was it Kiara who captivated him and
not one of the interns?

Wyatt had no time to ponder this because Kiara had
reached his side.

She leaned over to fill his glass and her fascinating
scent went straight to his head. She smelled honest,
clean—like wildflowers and sunshine and oatmeal.
She'd had oatmeal for breakfast.

Wyatt had been born with a heightened olfactory
sense. For years his family had thought that with his

talent for identifying the fine layers of scents, for sure he'd go into the wine business. But Wyatt was a bit of a rebel. He never did what was expected of him. Besides, there was a whole world out there to explore. Why confine oneself to a single profession?

He flattened his palms against the table.

His sense of that moment unfolded vividly and slowly as he clocked everything—the brush of her hand against his shoulder, the warmth of her body turning to slip between the two chairs, the sound of her breathing so quiet and even. He didn't see her so much as feel her.

A thought, unexpected and shocking, embedded in his brain.

This woman. She's the one.

And then she was gone, moving away, leaving him feeling bereft and adrift as she made her way back to the other side of the table where she'd started.

Alarmed, Wyatt shook his head, tried to empty her from his thoughts. What the hell was this? He wasn't the kind of guy who put claims on a woman. Everyone knew that. Wyatt DeSalme was footloose and fancy-free and...

He could not stop staring at Kiara Romano. Forcefully, he pried his gaze from her, made himself listen to Maurice, who had launched into the history and traditions of Bella Notte and how important interns were in the production of their wines.

Wyatt read between the lines. While under Kiara's management, Bella Notte's wines might be making a splash, but the small vineyard was still cash-strapped to the point where they depended on the free labor of interns to make ends meet. His brothers would gleefully rub their hands together at this bit of information. Bella

Notte was vulnerable financially, just as Scott and Eric had suspected, and he was here to deliver the crippling blow.

But that thought, which had excited him this morning because his brothers were finally taking him seriously, was bothersome, and he had no idea why. The Romanos were nothing to him except DeSalme competition. This was just business, a little underhanded espionage to expose the enemy's weakness. It was perfectly legal—as long as certain lines weren't crossed—and was done every single day of the week in corporate America.

So why did Wyatt feel the need to take a long, hot, soapy shower and scrub his soul clean?

After the wines were poured, Maurice passed out index cards and pens. Kiara stood beside the sideboard, assessing the assembled interns. Wyatt could feel the heat of her gaze on him.

He glanced up. A frown creased her lips.

"You are about to taste the three top wines produced by Bella Notte. Taste the white wine first," Maurice said, "and then write your impression on the card. Do not compare notes."

Wyatt thought it was odd to have the interns in for a wine tasting at eight in the morning, but what the hell? He cradled the wine glass in his hand, swirling it around and inhaled the fruity aroma.

Not the usual chardonnay, which gladdened his heart. Chardonnay was so overdone in California. Instead, Bella Notte's riesling delighted him—light, fresh and bright as a summer day.

One sip had him thinking of swimming pools and fireworks and homemade ice cream. The wine was a carousel ride, the taste intensifying as it rolled over his tongue and then ending humbly but sweetly on a gentle note.

He used the twenty-point Davis wine-ranking scale he'd been introduced to as a child. The riesling was a solid sixteen. No defects.

"Now for the cabernet," Maurice directed.

Wyatt closed his eyes and let his nose do the assessment first, identifying the individual notes—peppery, oaken without the obligatory smokiness and, just underneath, he caught a whiff of cherry, muted, but it was there.

He lifted the glass to his lips. The liquid slid smoothly over his tongue, then rushed up to greet his palate. It was a simple cab, yet noble and pristine. Purer than anything DeSalme produced. More intimate too.

The interns around him scribbled madly on their index cards, but Wyatt took his time, allowing the wine to resonate on the back of his tongue before finishing his assessment.

It was hauntingly delicate. A quality he'd never associated with a cab, but he couldn't decide whether it was indeed a quality that he wanted in a heavy red wine.

Everyone was making appreciative noises and Maurice had to remind them not to compare notes. Was he testing their abilities to describe wine? Or was he looking for a particular discernment of the taste buds?

Wyatt slid another glance over at Kiara. She was still staring at him. He held her gaze this time, refusing to look away. If she knew who he was, then she was going to have to call him out. Right here in front of everyone.

"And now," Maurice said, "for the wine that's going to take first place at the annual Sonoma Wine Festival next month…" He trailed off, paused dramatically.

Okay, nothing humble about that boast.

"I give you Bella Notte's premium dessert wine." He raised his hand like a stop sign. "But hold up a second. You must eat it with the chocolate lava cake baked by my Grandmother Romano to truly appreciate the joy that is Decadent Midnight."

The back door opened again and a wizened woman appeared carrying a tray of twenty-four teacup-size lava cakes, fresh from the oven, still steaming-hot. The smell of fine chocolate mingled with the aroma of wine.

This then, was the wine DeSalme had been hearing rumors about, the wine that was allegedly going to dethrone them as the reigning kings of Sonoma's Best of the Best Award. The wine that had caused his brothers to call him up in Greece and beg him to go undercover as an intern at Bella Notte.

Wyatt couldn't wait to drink it. He might not officially be in the family wine business, but he was an expert on luxury. Good food, good wine, good times were the tenets he lived by.

Grandma Romano settled a lava cake in front of him and a current of excitement ran around the table. Everyone was waiting for a cue from Maurice to begin.

But it was Kiara who picked up a narrow glass of the dark-purple dessert wine and raised it in the air. "Salut."

The group raised their glasses and echoed, "Salut."

The interns exchanged glances and grins, and then inhaled the intoxicating bouquet. It smelled like plums ripening in the sun. Wyatt thought immediately of Portugal and their port wines. But this was not a fortified wine.

Wyatt closed his eyes again. He heard forks clinking against china, the accompanying moans of pleasure, but he blocked all that out to focus exclusively on his own experience.

A late-harvest muscat. But this was more than a simple muscat. This wine was richer, truer. Not a false note anywhere.

First he tasted the concentrated melancholy sweetness, immediately followed by a kick of tingling warmth so surprising, his breath came out in a sharp, quick exhalation. Then the supreme flavor of pecan tiptoed in.

He opened his eyes and there was Kiara Romano, her stare cutting through him like a laser drill. To hide his guilt and his pleasure, he forked in a bite of hot gooey lava cake.

And that's when magic exploded inside his mouth.

Had he died and gone to epicurean heaven? His brain searched for a word respectful enough to describe the sensation but there simply were none.

Time hung suspended, a precious moment he'd never have again—the first time he tasted the true flavor of decadence.

Seconds? Minutes? An hour?

The pleasure was so barbarically beautiful he didn't ever want it to end. It tasted like the most sublime sin, and to think that the frumpily dressed woman with the smart green eyes was responsible for this…this…thing of sheer perfection.

His tongue slipped through the comingling of wine and chocolate—sweet and wet and hot. The combination of lava cake and Decadent Midnight rivaled great sex. He found the comparison surprising, but apt. It was all pure, thick, oozy pleasure. He'd never felt so giddy over a wine.

With every sip, as the indulgent notes tumbled and

rolled over his taste buds, his appreciation grew. A symphony. There was a virtual symphony in his mouth. It tasted like Vivaldi's "Autumn"—eager, crisp and rapturous, but underneath a haunting melancholia for things that could not last. Figs and apricots and musky late-autumn piqued his tongue. The wine's dark flesh caressed his throat. In that moment he was one-hundred-percent fully alive.

It was jaw-dropping, heart-stopping extraordinary wine of profound and complex character. A well-deserved twenty on the Davis scale. Wyatt's eyes flew open and he grabbed his pen and began to write, his hand barely able to keep up with his thoughts. It was almost as if he was channeling Bacchus, spewing his impressions on the index card in the pell-mell hurry reserved for people rushing to catch a flight just as the airplane doors were closing.

His brothers were right to be worried about the competition from Bella Notte Vineyards, and unless they could find Kiara Romano's Achilles' heel and get her to drop out of the contest, Decadent Midnight *was* going to thrash not only DeSalme in the Best of the Best Award—but every other wine in its category.

Happiness lingered on his tongue. A sweet skin of unforgettable sensation. He felt as if he'd just lost his virginity and couldn't wait to go back for more.

The beautiful wine had what the French called *terroir:* taste with a true sense of place. It tasted like where it was grown. Idyllic.

A hedonist's wet dream.

Everyone else had finished writing, but Wyatt couldn't seem to stop. Words fell, rain on the page, rushing to express his appreciation for Kiara's wine.

When he'd finally filled the entire note card, front to back, he set down his pen and looked around.

At some point during his purge of words, the blonde intern had gotten up and Kiara Romano had taken her seat. She studied him from across the table. Her eyes bright, shoulders thrust forward, chin quivering.

He smiled at her.

She blinked, a glazed, blissed-out expression shading her eyes. A smile identical to his own just-made-love grin curled at her lips.

With one swift motion, she pushed back her chair, then stood up and held out her hand.

"You," she commanded. "You come with me."

2

---

*Acidity: The tangy element in wine that
makes it feel bright, crisp and lively.*

THE MAN WAS perfect.

Too perfect.

He set off all Kiara's internal alarm bells. She did
not trust perfect.

Kiara led the way down the corridor. She heard the
sound of his sneakers slapping against the terrazzo
floor. As a natural introvert, she didn't particularly care
for this part of her job. Welcoming the interns, being all
warm and fuzzy and inviting when all she wanted was
to scuttle back to her quiet lab or the peaceful vineyards.
Maurice was good at the public relationships aspect of
running a winery. Kiara was not.

But she was the one who needed an assistant—her
family had finally convinced her to delegate some of the
lab duties—and the man behind her had demonstrated
all the essential qualities. Without an accomplished
assistant, she wasn't free to concentrate on her goal—
creating premium dessert wine that would turn Bella

Notte into the go-to vineyard for sweet, late-harvest wines of superior quality.

Her approach to winemaking differed from all the Romanos who had come before her. With a PhD in Viticulture and Enology, she was one-hundred-percent scientific. She kept excellent data. She played by the rules. No loosey-goosey, artsy "magic" of winemaking for her. Yes, Great-grandfather Romano had achieved a lot in his day with nothing but natural talent and grapevines nurtured all the way across the ocean from Naples, but time and technology had changed winemaking from instinct to a discipline.

Now for the nitty-gritty of the interview.

Don't get your hopes up, just because this guy seems to have all the traits you're looking for. Take your time. There's no rush.

It sounded good, but that wasn't true. She'd managed to pluck Bella Notte from the brink of bankruptcy after her father's illness had forced him to step down as head of the winery, but they were still far from secure. Decadent Midnight, her own creation, was the ace in the hole and this year it was her chance to shine at the Sonoma Best of the Best competition.

She pushed through the door into her lab. She waved at a metal stool drawn up to one of the tables. "Have a seat."

Kiara went around to the other side of the table, but remained standing. Folding her arms over her chest, she canted her head, studying the man.

Behind the dark-framed glasses he wore, eyes the deep color of chestnuts stared back at her. Brown shaggy hair flopped over his forehead, giving him a rakish appearance. He looked as though he dressed with the help of a thrift store. Nothing wrong with that. Between being young and either in college or just graduated, most interns were broke.

But beneath the surface, this guy was different.

For one thing, his nails were buffed and he had no calluses on his palms, unlike her work-roughened hands. Plus, he moved with an air of self-confidence that belied his position. And then there was his clear talent for evaluating wine. Why hadn't another winery snapped him up by now?

Maurice handled the intern applications and training. Where had her cousin found him?

Her eyes met his.

A slow, easy grin started at one side of his mouth and slipped to the other while his gaze cockleburred onto hers.

Slick. He was way too slick.

Kiara scowled.

His smile teetered and for a flash of a second, she saw hesitation in his face and she immediately liked him better.

Maybe the bravado was all show. Maybe he wasn't as cocky as he seemed. Or maybe she was simply too wary. Her whole family told her she should be more open, more trusting, more romantic, like her sister, Deirdre. Easy for them to say. Love for them prevented her from pointing out that their trust of an unscrupulous accountant had placed the Romanos' livelihood in serious jeopardy and crusty ol' Kiara was the one who had to save them.

"I'm Kiara." She thrust out her hand.

The smile returned. "So I heard." He took her hand. "Wyatt Jordan."

The instant their hands touched a blast of raw sexual desire shot up her arm and sped a blistering trail straight to her groin. Her body reacting to him without her approval: that had never happened before

Wyatt's eyes widened.

Kiara withdrew her hand, her gaze dropping to her feet.

Silence crawled by, slow and painful.

"So…" she said, ignoring the butterfly storm in her stomach.

"So," he echoed.

"Looks like we both have the same extensive vocabulary."

"Regular Groliers, us two."

He was funny. And smart. Dangerous combo. Don't forget gorgeous. See. Too perfect.

This time, she noticed the shape of his lips. Angular. Wide and welcoming. Very kissable lips. Helplessly, she felt her attraction to him grow. This was definitely out of the ordinary for her. She wasn't the kind of woman who did anything heedlessly, much less indulged in lusty impulses, but she could not stop herself from tracking down his strong masculine chin, to his broad shoulders and chest. Good thing he was sitting behind a table, otherwise, she would have been tempted to let her gaze stroll even lower.

What in the hell was wrong with her? She needed to take control of the situation, and take control of it now.

"I have another taste test I want to give you," she said.

"Bring it."

She held up one finger. "I'll be right back."

Kiara took off from the lab, more as an excuse to

compose herself than anything else. This intern had potential, but her physical reaction to him scared her. She needed to make sure he was the one before she offered him the job as her assistant. She had a test in mind to see if he really did have a discerning tongue and olfactory sense or if he was just a great pretender. She suspected the latter.

When she was in grad school, she'd been involved in a study based on a blind taste test featuring two name-brand colas. In the original experiment, all the blindfolded participants preferred the taste of the lesser-known brand to the best-selling soda. The researchers wanted to understand why the best-tasting cola was not the best-selling cola so they did a second test where they performed an MRI on the subjects as they drank the colas and discovered the "reward" center of the brain lit up when they drank the lesser-known brand.

In a clever twist, the researchers repeated the experiment a third time, informing the participants that they were drinking the name brand even though they were not. This time their brains lit up in the "reward" region, the same as they had previously done with the brand whose flavor they had enjoyed more.

Kiara's scientific mind found the results of this experiment both fascinating and frustrating. It meant that for most people, brand loyalty trumped quality. Given human psychology, how did an upstart winery compete against the big labels? It was a question that had plagued her for years, but now that she was in charge of Bella Notte it had become the paramount question.

She needed something—*someone*—to help her bridge the gap between the myth of a name brand's superiority and the science of truly good wine. She had to believe that some level of objectivity could be found and exploited.

But how?

Test this guy. See if he truly is discerning enough to differentiate between taste and brand.

All right, so it was a bit underhanded. She'd admit it. But if she was going to let this guy into her lab, take him on as an assistant, she needed some assurance he was the real deal.

Or was she simply kidding herself? Was she just trying to find an excuse to keep the super-hot guy around?

Kiara's cheeks flushed. No, no, that wasn't what she was doing. She wasn't the kind of person who allowed something like sexual attraction get in the way of her goals. She wanted him because he had exhibited a rare talent for detecting the subtle smells and flavors of wine.

She was focused. Resolute. Her goal was single-minded and lofty. Consistently produce the best dessert wine in California, and if Wyatt Jordan could help her do that, well then, she would use him.

Yeah? So why are you standing out here in the corridor?

She shook her head and took the steps down to the wine cellar. The cool, earthy smell enveloped her. She loved it down here in this old-fashioned cellar with stone walls and a floor of ram-packed earth. When she was a child, this had been her favorite place to play. She'd learned to read down here at age four, spelling out the letters on the wine labels. In the cellar, she felt especially linked to her family, to the past, to the entire history of winemaking. It was an ancient, provocative lure.

Rows and rows of wine racks provided an intriguing honeycomb of product. Most of it, of course, was Bella Notte harvest, but they did keep competitors' wines on hand as well. Kiara visited that section of the cellar and stood studying the options—Mondavi, Gallo, DeSalme.

Hmm. DeSalme made a red dessert muscat in the vein of—but certainly not in the league of—Decadent Midnight. She'd use it for the comparison.

She took a bottle of the DeSalme wine, along with a bottle of Decadent Midnight, went up the back stairs and into the family kitchen. Once there, she poured the DeSalme wine into a glass pitcher, filled the empty bottle of DeSalme muscat with Decadent Midnight and then transferred the DeSalme wine from the glass pitcher into the Bella Notte bottle. She replaced the corks in each bottle and then hurried back to the lab. If the man waiting in her lab could tell the difference between the DeSalme muscat and Decadent Midnight, then he truly was the person she'd been searching for.

If not, she would dispatch him to the vineyards with the other interns, never to darken the door of her lab again.

THE INSTANT KIARA returned into the lab carrying the bottle of DeSalme wine fear seized Wyatt.

Uh-oh. This wasn't good. Not good at all.

Busted.

The determined expression on her face made his heart cringe. What to say? His tongue curled around a lie.

How had Kiara figured out who he was? Had he somehow tipped his hand? Had he inadvertently revealed too much knowledge of wine? Eric and Scott would razz the hell out of him for getting bounced from Bella Notte this quickly. And he would deserve it. God, he hated being a bumbler in his brothers' eyes.

Bluff. Just bluff your way through this. Bluff and deny, deny, deny.

Her gaze met his and the strangest sensation swept over him. As if he were being led to his doom and he couldn't wait to get there.

Wyatt's pulse rate quickened. What was up? What game was she playing? Why not just confront him? He moistened his lips.

C'mon, think of a line. Something brilliant to deflect her anger, but hell if he didn't come up empty, his eyes too full of Kiara to process anything else. Anything beyond the sight of her oval face and abundance of corkscrew auburn curls escaping madly from her loose ponytail.

He started working on an excuse in his head, planning how he'd charm and disarm her when she confronted him as a spy. He would cock his head, let his famous grin slowly steal across his face and peer deep into her eyes as if she were the only woman on the face of the earth. The technique never failed to buckle the knees of women both young and old.

"Hand me those two glasses." She nodded at two wineglasses perched on a shelf to his right.

Was he being led into a trap? Congenially, he reached for the glasses, and then set them down on the lab table in front of her.

Kiara pulled the corkscrew from her pocket, uncorked both bottles of wine. One DeSalme's. The other Decadent Midnight.

Corks popped, smooth and cool, and the air carried

a musty, yeasty smell of fermented grapes. She tipped two ounces of DeSalme into one glass, two ounces of Decadent Midnight in the other.

"Another taste test," she told him. "Comparison."

He caressed her gaze. More from instinct than ploy. What was going on here? If she knew he was a fraud, why not just toss him out on his ass? Why the games? And why did he feel like a skiff adrift in an ocean squall?

"Sure," he said, nice and easy. Gave her that aw-shucks shrug he'd perfected. Cool as ice on a summer's day.

"Why are you looking at me like that?" she snapped. She had a great voice, even when she was angry—especially when she was angry—all deep and husky.

Wyatt blinked, widened his grin, making sure his dimples were showing. What was wrong? Maybe it was the glasses. Girls don't make passes at guys who wear glasses? Even girls who also wore glasses. Was that it? He thought about whipping them off, then reconsidered.

"What's the matter with you?" she asked. "Are you impaired?"

Feeling rattled, he stood up, stepped toward her. His smile faltered, but he caught it like a teetering grocery-store display and pasted it back in place. There. Unfazed.

"Taste." She commanded, pushing the glass with the DeSalme wine in it toward him.

Tension pulled taut in his gut. This was wacky, weird, wonky. He picked up the glass, his nose twitching at the melancholy smell.

"Bouquet," she commanded.

Okay, if that's the way it was going to be, he could

handle a little rough and tumble. He nailed her with his eyes and they stepped into a silent, motionless waltz.

"Supple," Wyatt said.

"What else?" Her pupils narrowed.

"Complex."

"And?" she nudged.

He half expected her to poke him with one of those long slender fingers. *Good God, she's magnificent.*

Wyatt's blood bloomed, fumed, and he had no idea why. She was not his usual type. Everything about her seemed foreign and strange and at the same time uniquely familiar. He yearned for her in a way he'd never yearned for another. Confused, he pushed his hair from his eyes and concentrated on his surroundings.

They were all alone in the womb of her laboratory. White lab jackets hung on wall pegs. The faint arcing and sparking smell of ozone curled in his nostrils. Beakers and test tubes, Bunson burners and pH-test kits, centrifuges and scales, rubber hoses and pipettes, tongs and stoppers and test-tube holders and evaporating dishes. Tall metal stools were pulled up to the stainless-steel lab table. But, while it was well stocked, most of the equipment looked outdated—probably purchased years ago—nothing like the high-tech corporate lab at DeSalme. This was a mom-and-pop operation all the way. It should be easy enough for DeSalme to crush Bella Notte

Guilt gnawed at the back of his brain and he felt a sudden urge to be on the side of David instead of Goliath.

"Well?" She was a pushy one.

"Surprising," Wyatt said, but he was not speaking of the wine.

"What else?"

"Mind-bending."

"Impertinent," she said.

"The wine?"

"You."

"But I intrigue you."

"Not you," she said. "Your tongue."

"Now who's being impertinent?"

Her cheeks reddened with effrontery. "I didn't mean it like that."

Finally. He'd rattled her.

She fumbled his gaze, turned to put on a lab jacket. *Professor* Vineyard Commando. He readied his grin, dialed it to stun.

Kiara turned back, held up a palm, a firm stop sign between them. "Look, clearly that I'm-so-handsome-that-it-hurts thing usually works well for you, but if you want this job, knock it off."

He tipped the glass to his lips let the liquid slip over his tongue.

Pow!

There it was again. That same sweet kick of pure pleasure that had stormed his senses back in the tasting room.

Wyatt glanced from his glass to the bottle she'd poured from. Yep. The DeSalme label. He lowered his lashes, studied Kiara for a long, hard moment. What was she trying to pull? This wasn't DeSalme's muscat. Something was up and he wasn't walking into her trap. He was going to make her call him out.

"Well?"

"I thought you wanted a comparison," he hedged.

She pursed her lips, but said nothing. She did have

an exceptionally gorgeous mouth. Full and lush. Like plump ripe grapes. "I do."

"I'll need a palate cleanser before I try the other wine."

She opened one of the table drawers, reached in and pulled out a packet of plain unsalted crackers. With one eyebrow arched upward in a skeptical expression, she passed him the crackers.

He took a bite. The soft crunch was the only sound in the room except for the ticking of the wall clock. The bland cracker soaked up the fruity taste of wine.

Kiara presented him the second glass of wine decanted from the Decadent Midnight bottle.

He swirled the liquid in the glass, inhaled.

"Bouquet?" she asked.

How was he going to play this? Straight up? Or coy? "Secretive," he said, going for coy and pulling out the double entendres.

Her eyes widened. "What else?"

His stare locked in on hers again. "Deceptively simple."

She squirmed. Surely she had to know she was busted. "And?"

"You really want to do this?" he asked, leaning across the table.

She tightened her jaw. The pulse at the hollow of her throat fluttered. He stared at the provocative stirring.

Her hand moved to cover the telltale spot. "Do what, Mr. Jordan?"

"Tango."

She drew in an audible breath. "I have no idea what you're talking about."

"Just tell me one thing. Why are you playing with me?"

A flash of emotion crossed her face and in that split second she looked achingly vulnerable, and that made him feel soft in the general vicinity of his heart. "You know?"

"That you switched the bottles? Of course I know. What I can't figure out is why." Except he did know why. She knew he was a DeSalme and she wanted to make him admit it. Well, he wasn't going to admit anything. She was going to have to accuse him.

Suddenly, startlingly, she grinned. A grin that made him feel like her hero.

Why was she grinning? It was a bit disorienting after all that hostility.

"Well, what do you know," she murmured, more to herself than to him. "A guy who speaks the truth."

Wyatt exhaled and it was only then he realized he'd been holding his breath, waiting for her to accuse him of being a DeSalme.

While he was relieved she hadn't unmasked him as DeSalme's mole, part of him felt disappointed. Not with her. But with himself for remaining silent.

"The truth?" he asked.

"You're a supertaster."

"A what?"

"You have the inherent ability to identify all the different notes in a wine. That's why I was testing you. A lot of people can talk a good game, but when you present them with the more expensive label, they invariably perceive it as the superior wine, no matter what's in the bottle. But you didn't fall for it."

"Seriously? Most people can't tell the difference?"

She told him about the experiment she'd performed as a research assistant in graduate school, something about competing cola brands, MRIs and the power of advertising. He understood that. He'd spent some time in the marketing department at DeSalme before deciding it wasn't for him.

"You didn't let the pricey DeSalme label fool you," she said. "I saw it on your face when you were drinking Decadent Midnight with Grandmamma's lava cake. It's a treasured talent, but I had to be sure you weren't just bluffing."

No kidding? Yes, he'd always had a knack for picking out the right wine with the right meal—sometimes friends would call him up while they were on dates and ask his advice on what wine to order—but he attributed the skill to his family's profession.

"What was the expression on my face?"

"And your comments on the note card," she went on. "You described the wine like you were reviewing Beethoven live at Carnegie Hall."

"What was the look on my face?" he persisted.

"It doesn't matter."

"If it doesn't matter, why don't you just tell me?"

"You have a hard time letting things go, don't you?"

"Not at all. I'm famous for letting things go. Girlfriends. Bad habits. Housekeepers. I have a hell of a time keeping housekeepers."

"You can afford a housekeeper?"

Most thirty-something guys working as interns couldn't afford housekeepers. He had to be careful. *Quick, stun her with your wit.* "No, that's why I can't keep them."

"Point taken."

Okay. He'd sidestepped that one. "So what was the face?"

Kiara sighed. "You lied about being good at letting things go."

"So sue me," he said. "I lied. What face?"

"Orgasmic," she said bluntly. "You had an orgasmic expression on your face. Happy now?"

Orgasmic? Had she actually said that? Damn. His cheeks burned. Thank God he had a heavy five-o'clock shadow or she would see that she'd caused him to blush. When was the last time he'd blushed? When had he *ever* blushed? Wyatt didn't have a bashful bone in his body. He did not blush. And yet, here he was, blushing.

"And that told you what?"

"You're very sensual."

"Well, all you had to do was ask. I could have told you that." His mother called it self-indulgent, but what was so wrong with sleeping on satin sheets? And what did she know? After she left the guy she'd left his father for, she hooked up with some Norwegian crab fisherman named Lars Bakke off the coast of Bear Butt, Alaska, or some such place, and started carving figurines out of animal bone.

"Do you know how long I've been searching for someone with your innate talent?"

"A long time?" he guessed.

"Years."

"Looks like today is your lucky day," he drawled.

Her smile disappeared and her lips pressed into a stern line. She glared. Funny, she looked adorable when she glared. And she glared a lot, so that meant she was pretty damned cute.

"Sorry," he apologized.

"If I accept you as an intern, you're going to be working here in the lab with me, Mr. Jordan. The rest of the interns will be out in the vineyards."

Well, now, that was a happy turn of events. He couldn't have planned this any better. She was inviting him right into the heart of her winery, into the nerve center, the inner sanctum. Privy to Bella Notte's best-kept secrets. He could do some serious damage here.

Maybe.

"Wyatt," he said.

"What?"

"Call me Wyatt."

"I'm a hard task master, Mr. Jordan. Winemaking is my passion, my life, my reason for being on this earth. I take it very seriously. I'm excited to have found someone with your wine-tasting talents, but if you can't do as I ask, when I ask you to do it, without any questions, then you're out on your keister. Got it?"

"Keister?" He tried not to laugh. Failed. "Sounds like something a vaudevillian would say."

She sank her hands on her hips. "It's a word. Look it up."

He resisted the urge to salute and say, "Aye, aye, Captain." Instead he toned down his smile. "You're the boss."

"You seem old for an intern."

"What can I say?" Wyatt spread his arms. "I'm a late bloomer. Misspent youth and all that."

"Trust-fund baby, huh?"

He startled. He thought he disguised himself pretty well, but she'd seen right through him. She had his number.

"Nah," he lied, surprised to find how uncomfortable lying to her made him feel. "Just a slacker."

Her frown deepened. "May I assume you've put those slacker tendencies behind you?"

To demonstrate his commitment, Wyatt started rolling up his sleeve. "I'm ready to work."

"You're a jokester."

"You're not."

"Mr. Jordan, you will do everything I ask of you, no questions asked."

"Yes."

"It was a statement," she said. "Not a question."

"Gotcha." Fiery. He liked that about her. In fact, he liked everything about her and it occurred to him that could be a serious problem.

"What did you study in college?" she asked.

"A little bit of this, a little bit of that."

"You're a dilettante."

"I prefer the term *renaissance man*." He winked, but that didn't work any better for him than his grin.

"Of course you do."

"Were you aware that you can be a tad dismissive?" he asked.

"Excuse me?"

"Oh, I get that you're too absorbed in winemaking for polite conversation, but you have a tendency to dismiss people out of hand if they don't immediately fall in line with your plan or live up to your expectations."

Dude, what are you doing? You're supposed to be winning her over, not pissing her off. You're here to spy on her, not call her on her less than positive traits.

Wyatt knew he should shut up, but he just kept rattling. "It's inconsiderate."

"You don't know anything about me."

"I know what I see."

She shifted, but seemed to give his comment some thought. "You're right. I have a tendency to get absorbed in my work and ignore everything else."

"Some might even say rude."

"Is that a criticism?"

"We've all got our flaws." He shrugged.

"Some of us more than others."

Did she mean herself or him?

Finally, she pulled out the chair beside him and sat down. "Why wine?" she quizzed. "What attracts you?"

He was about to say something glib, like, "Why not?" Or "What better way to spend the day than drinking wine?" But he got the distinct impression such a tongue-in-cheek response was not what she was looking for from a potential intern, and he needed to correct the bad impression he'd made. "I believe that to master something so complex and engrossing would be a life well spent."

She folded her arms across her chest, eyed him speculatively as if gauging his response on her internal bullshit meter. Kiara Romano was a tough nut to crack.

"Besides," he said, unable to resist his natural inclination to tease. "There's nothing more romantic than the art of making wine."

She held up her palm. She used the gesture liberally. "Let me stop you right there."

"What?"

"Winemaking is *not* an art. That's a dreamy, illogical, magical supposition and it has no place in *my* laboratory. Winemaking is a science that can be measured and controlled. It's quantitative and qualitative. It's the human perception of wine that's faulty."

"Okay." Clearly, he'd punched one of her hot buttons.

"That silly legend you've heard floating around Idyll is pure poppycock and it's only useful as a marketing tool for people who like to believe in romantic nonsense."

"Poppycock." He pantomimed writing it on a notepad. "Gotcha."

"I'm a scientist. My focus is science. If my cousin Maurice can increase our customer base by capitalizing on a fable, well, more power to him. Me, I prefer to concentrate on using proven scientific techniques to produce the best wine possible."

He held up an index finger and thumb, measuring off an inch. "You don't think that there is at least a little bit of magic in the—"

"No," she said sharply. "And if you want to work for me, you won't bring that up again."

All rightee then. Message received. Not a romantic bone in her body. "No more romantic poppycock."

"You're making fun of me."

"I have to. You're just too serious and I get the feeling you have most of the people around here buffaloed."

"I have to be tough." She notched up her chin.

"Only on the outside. I can tell that on the inside you melt like a Popsicle in the sun."

"Seriously? Women go for stuff like this?"

"Oh, yeah."

She snorted and rolled her eyes but he could tell that underneath she wanted to smile, just somewhere along the way she'd come up with the notion that allowing herself to relax and enjoy herself meant she was weak or something.

"Now," she said. "You can return to the group. Maurice will give you a tour of the winery and then show you to your accommodations. Get settled in and then be back in here tomorrow morning at seven o'clock on the dot and be prepared to work hard."

"On the dot." Wyatt tried his grin again, but she wasn't going for it.

She made him feel…well…like the punch line of a big joke. It wasn't often a woman sliced right through his easygoing demeanor. He was accustomed to women cutting him all kinds of slack, laughing at his jokes, letting him off the hook.

But not Kiara. She seemed as if she was severely disappointed in him, but determined to make the best of an unsatisfactory situation.

Kiara's disdain made Wyatt yearn all the more to impress her and he marveled how such a tart-tongued woman had created a wine as sweet as Decadent Midnight.

He had a sudden urge to tell her who he was, why he was here, to beg her forgiveness and then ask her out on a date. He opened his mouth. Almost confessed.

He could imagine hearing his brother Scott saying, "We can never depend on Wyatt. When it comes to a choice between business or a woman, he'll choose the woman every time."

Right. Wyatt closed his mouth, swallowed the impulse. His brothers had given him a chance to prove himself and he wasn't about to let a woman—no matter how intriguing—screw with his head.

3

Complex: A wine that has many different flavors and facets.

KIARA STOOD ON the small patio outside her lab watching Maurice herd the interns back into the vans. Her gaze hung on Wyatt's tall frame and an uneasy prickling sensation tickled the back of her neck. She let out a long sigh and poked both hands into the pockets of her apron.

Great. Just her luck. She'd finally found an intern with an acute sense of taste and smell, and a strong discernment for the complexity of quality wine, and he turned out to be a charming, smart-aleck slacker. Wyatt had an oozy grin that said he used it often to get out of trouble. The shaggy, unkempt hair and scraggly stubble told her he was too lazy for a proper haircut and daily shave. He was rumpled, slovenly and…and…

He'd boldly called her on her flaws. That was irritating and unexpected, but he was right. She did tend to dismiss people who didn't do things her ways. It was a flaw she'd been working on correcting. Frequently, she had to remind herself that not everyone believed the way she believed or valued the things she valued—like family, hard work and holding on to one's ideals.

But there was a part of her that wondered how different her life would have been if she'd followed a different path, hadn't held herself to such high standards.

The man's good for you. He challenges you. Keeps you on your toes. And he could teach you how not to take yourself so seriously.

Wyatt carried himself with supreme self-confidence. Cocky. In spite of the thick, dark-framed glasses, he was good-looking and he knew it. The guy was giving off mixed messages and as much as she hated to admit it, he intrigued her.

She gritted her teeth.

No. Just no.

She was not even going to go there. Never mind that her hand still tingled from where she'd grabbed his wrist and dragged him into the lab. Any kind of attraction to her intern was not only absurd but inappropriate as well.

Shaking her head to empty it of unwanted thoughts, she went back into the lab. She had work to do. No time for daydreaming over Wyatt Jordan. Before she could shut the door, a silky black cat that had shown up at the winery a few days earlier darted inside. She'd fed him and apparently she now belonged to him. If she was going to keep the cat, she needed to make an appointment with the vet. She had a soft spot for animals.

Kiara bent to scoop him into her arms. "You are the only charming male I'm letting into my life, Felix."

The cat purred and snuggled up against her neck.

"Yes, okay, I'll admit it. I'm a sucker for cute, hairy guys. You're in. But you can't let word get out that I'm such a soft touch. I've worked hard on building this game face. You don't get to be head of a winery by being a pushover, even if it *is* the family business. As for Wyatt Jordan, I'm definitely on the fence about him. He's got tasting talent, but not much of a work ethic."

Felix meowed.

"Oh, so you're on his side? Guys stick together, is that it?" Kiara scratched the cat behind his ears. "The truth is, I need him. Yes, our wines are getting good press, but it costs a lot of money to make a run for the top against the big boys like DeSalme and Mondavi. Decadent Midnight is my ace in the hole. If we win the Sonoma Best of the Best Award…well…things will change around here. But for now, we're pretty well flat broke."

Felix meowed again.

"Don't get distressed. We have enough to cover cat food, but honestly, if it weren't for these interns, I couldn't make ends meet. But you, my dear, do not belong in a lab." Still cradling Felix, Kiara opened the side door and carried the cat into her apartment directly adjacent to the laboratory. She opened the cabinet, scooped kibble from the sack of cat food she'd bought last week.

"And then there's the issue that any of them could go blabbing to our competition," she continued her one-sided conversation. "Yes, the interns will sign a confidentiality agreement, but money talks and if someone like DeSalme woos them away, we're in trouble."

She poured the kibble into a blue plastic bowl and

sat Felix down so he could have at his breakfast. The cat's soft crunching was the only sound in the room.

"Yes," Kiara said. "You're right. We need to keep our interns happy."

Especially an intern with Wyatt's talent.

He made her feel things she shouldn't feel. Emotion. That was the problem. It was *always* the problem. A good scientist did not allow emotions to sway her. A good scientist tucked her feelings away. A good scientist relied on her brain, not her heart.

But like it or not, she needed him if she wanted to continue to improve her wine and grow her market base. Producing complexly nuanced wines was the best way to do that and Wyatt could help her get there.

The trick? Keep him close while at the same time keeping the attraction she felt for him under tight control, because the last thing she needed right now was any kind of romantic entanglement.

DORMITORIES.

Wow. Wyatt had never lived in a dormitory, not even during his brief stint in college.

Maurice Romano had given the interns a five-hour tour of the winery, complete with a picnic lunch in the vineyards. Then they'd walked to the back of the property, a good fifteen-minute hike from the main house, to the intern accommodations.

The building was quaint—he'd give it that—an old stone farmhouse sitting at the edge of the vineyards.

"Two to a room," Maurice called out. "The kitchen and bathrooms are communal and you're expected to keep them clean. There's a list of rotation duties posted on the corkboard in the hallway. Spend the rest of the day getting acclimated to your new surroundings. You'll hit the ground running tomorrow morning."

Great. He was going to have a roommate as well. This was not what he'd signed up for.

Quit your bitchin', DeSalme. You're in. You're golden. You're a supertaster. You've got free run of the lab. Your brothers will love you for it. Besides you get to hang out with Kiara. Life is good.

"Wanna room together?" asked a whippet-lean kid barely in his twenties, looking all surf-bum cool with long blond hair and a nutmeg tan.

"Yeah, sure." Wyatt shrugged. Go with the flow. That motto had served him well over the years.

"Steve." The kid stuck out his hand. "Steve Harmon."

"Wyatt." He shook the kid's hand. "De…er…Jordan."

Oops, almost flubbed. He had to be careful. This was his opportunity to prove once and for all that he was as capable as his older brothers. His family had always marginalized him and he'd allowed it to happen. *Oh, that's just Wyatt. Pretty-boy Wyatt. Little brother's all charm and no substance.*

Okay, yes. It had taken him some time to find himself. A year of backpacking through Europe with a group of buddies hadn't done it, although his knack for fun and adventure had landed him a job in Italy as a Ferrari salesman. He'd made salesman of the year before a wealthy older woman coaxed him to come work for her advertising agency in Paris. That gig hadn't lasted long because hey, he was no gigolo. But the ad agency gave him the cache he needed to do public relations for a company that built yachts. He stayed there three years. Then he became enchanted with a dark-eyed Greek girl, bought his own yacht at a deep discount and sailed to

Greece to be with her. That love affair had last all of six weeks, but his love affair with Greece had blossomed. He'd been living in a condo in Athens for the past two years, working when it suited him, contracting on PR jobs, including doing some work for his brothers. And as soon as he was around them again, the teasing resumed. They called him Peter Pan. Said he would never grow up.

He acted as if he didn't care, and for most of his life he'd convinced himself that he wasn't bothered by their lack of respect, but lately—well, hell, it had been his thirty-first birthday, hadn't it, that had made him start looking at things differently? That and his last girlfriend's pregnancy scare the previous summer.

He'd liked Heather well enough, but not any more than any of his other girlfriends. She'd been a graduate student from the University of Iowa in Greece for the summer. They'd had a helluva good time, keeping things light, just as they both wanted it.

And then Heather had missed her period.

Heather had freaked out. Wyatt had thought he would freak. He'd always imagined he would freak out in any kind of situation that promised to tie him down, but instead, he'd actually been surprisingly excited about the prospect of becoming a dad. Now *that* had scared him.

The potential baby turned out to be a false alarm. He and Heather had both breathed a sigh of relief and had gone their separate ways, but in the back of his mind a seed of an idea had been planted. An idea he'd done his best to ignore for the past year until Scott had called him and asked him to go undercover at Bella Notte.

His brother had finally asked for his help. For the first time, he'd really felt like part of the business.

He liked the feeling. Another surprise.

Wyatt and his new roomie walked to the last room unclaimed by the other interns. Steve opened the door.

Bunk beds. Seriously?

"I get the top," Steve declared and slung himself onto the top bunk.

"Be my guest," Wyatt said.

"Dude, what happened when the scary-looking chick took you into the back room? We were all wondering if you'd gotten thrown out already."

Scary-looking? For some reason the comment rankled. Just because a woman was strong and independent didn't mean she was scary.

Ha, how many strong, independent women have you dated?

Okay, so he preferred his females on the fun-loving, compliant side. That didn't mean he couldn't appreciate Kiara for who she was.

"Kiara Romano runs Bella Notte. Show a little respect."

"Whoa." Steve held up both palms. "I didn't know you were into her. My bad."

"I'm not *into* her."

"Sure you're not."

Maybe he'd made a mistake in teaming up with surfer boy here. "What makes you say that?"

"I dunno." Steve laced his fingers, cradled the back of his head in his palms. "You kept looking at her like she's a puzzle you can't wait to solve."

Did he? "Funny," Wyatt said. "You don't look like the philosophical type."

"It's sumpthin' my mom says," he admitted.

"In other words, you have no idea what you're talking about."

"None whatsoever," Steve said good-naturedly. "Me, I'm intrigued by the little blonde."

"You mean Lauren?"

"Yeah." Steve smiled dreamily. "Great tits."

"She's out of your league."

"No doubt. Doesn't stop a guy from dreamin'."

No, no it didn't. An odd edginess pushed Wyatt toward the curtainless window. From this vantage point, he could see the slope but not the top of Twin Hearts.

"So, since Kiara Romano didn't vote you off the island, what was that secret meeting about?"

"She had me taste more wine."

"Is she looking to hook up with you?" Steve swung down off the bunk and went to join Wyatt at the window.

"Huh?"

"You know. Summer intern fling. It's done all the time."

Was it? "No. She offered me a position working with her in the lab."

Steve poked Wyatt with his elbow. "That's it, dude. You're not reading the signs. She's picked you for her lover."

Had she? That startled him and for one foolish moment he felt pleased. Then common sense prevailed. Kiara had not been impressed with him in the least. His one saving grace was his ability to distinguish multi layers of taste in wine and describe them vividly. The kid had a screw loose and Wyatt was dumb for giving any credence to anything he said.

"What *are* you talking about?" Wyatt asked. "We're here to lean about grapes, not to hook up."

He could hardly believe he was saying this. Not so long ago, his thoughts would have been traveling the same path as Steve's. But now? Hell, he didn't know. Jumbled. His mind was jumbled and it was all Kiara's fault. She turned him upside down.

"You know. Like Susan Sarandon's character in *Bull Durham*. She picked baseball players to have sex with during the season, then dumped them when the summer's over. I heard it's the same at wineries. Vineyard interns get all kinds of tail. That's why I'm here."

"What *have* you been smoking?"

Steve laughed. "I'm serious."

"You're just here to chase women?" Actually, from a young stud's viewpoint it made sense—lots of young people, summer employment, beautiful setting with a romantic legend equaled hot, casual sex. Wyatt's chest grew tight and warm just thinking about it. "You're not interested in wine?"

"Hell, yeah. I love drinking the stuff."

"You do know you're going to have to work?" Why was he lecturing the kid? Since when did Wyatt ever crack the whip? Still, the guy was so immature. *Remind you of anyone?* "And you don't get paid a salary."

"It'll be worth it," Steve said, flopping on his bunk again and cradling his head in his palms. "I can't wait to see those girls bending over the grapevines."

Wyatt suppressed an eye roll. Boys would be boys. Since when did he ever judge someone for the way they lived their lives? He got enough of that kind of indictment from his family. He wasn't about to start dishing it out.

IT WAS FIVE minutes after seven the following morning when Wyatt sauntered into Kiara's lab to find her standing at the top of a ladder, underneath the smoke alarm, a nine-volt battery clutched in her hand.

"You're late," she announced and pointed at the clock, not bothering with a civil greeting.

For the past two mornings in a row he'd gotten up at the crack of dawn, not his favorite time of day. Wyatt preferred twilight to dawn. Sunset to sunrise. When he was a kid, before his parents had divorced, his mother would send the maid up to bang pots and pans together to force him from the bed. He had to admit he'd been something of a jackass as a teen—lazy, undisciplined, bestowing a killer grin on the world to get his way.

Wyatt shrugged. "The walk from the dormitory took longer than I expected."

"No excuses. Late is late."

"You can dock my pay." He dusted off the women-slaying grin.

Kiara glowered. She was really good at glowering. No wonder Steve had described her as the scary-looking chick. But Wyatt saw past the fierceness. She had a lot on her shoulders. She ran a winery. People depended on her. She didn't have the time or patience for horsing around.

Wyatt felt a twinge of sympathy and put away his smile. Did she ever get to relax, enjoy her own wines, and have a good time? "Do you need some help with that?"

"No," she said curtly. "I do not."

He traced his gaze up her bare calf to the hem of her unflattering dress. It looked almost identical to the one she had on the day before. But even the frumpy dress couldn't cloak the fact that the woman possessed an awesome pair of legs. A sweet shimmering sizzle started in his gut and spread slowly throughout his limbs.

This was nuts. Stop thinking about her legs.

Wyatt shifted his attention to the ladder. "Your ladder looks precarious. How old is it?"

"It's older than I am, but it's fine. Don't worry about me. I don't need you to worry about me."

"How about if I just hold—" He stepped closer.

"I said I'm fine," she barked.

He raised both palms, backed off. Sheesh, if she were an animal she'd be a pit bull. "Are you always this testy?"

"When there's an annoying intern who can't show up on time buzzing around me asking irritating questions, yes, I'm always this testy."

Wyatt chortled.

Kiara snorted and leaned over too far in order to reach the smoke detector.

"Look out." Wyatt rushed over to steady the ladder.

But it was too late. Gravity already had ahold of her and momentum took her down. The ladder stayed secure in Wyatt's grip, but Kiara lurched sideways.

He grabbed for her and felt his own equilibrium shift.

The ladder scooted across the terrazzo tile. Kiara tumbled free, falling into his arms and knocking him flat onto his backside.

Reflexively, he curled his arms around her waist, folding her protectively to his chest. She knocked the pins out from under him. Literally. He was smack on his butt, Kiara cradled against him.

Gotcha.

Their gazes met.

Glued.

Her eyes rounded wide and she started to draw back, but he wasn't about to let her go. He saw on her face the same baffled attraction that seized him like a sudden chokehold.

"The ground moved," she said.

Hallelujah to that.

Good God, but she was a showstopper. Beyond that overgrowth of unruly curls were the most intelligent eyes he'd ever had the pleasure of falling into and Wyatt had fallen into the pool of many an attractive woman's gaze. Not to mention that she smelled really good too— like cotton and soap and strawberries.

For a long second, it seemed they were frozen in place, their bodies plastered together. His arms wrapped around her. Her gaze grafted to his. Their lips so damned close it ought to be illegal.

If he kissed her, what would she taste like? Grapes? Or something deeper, more exotic?

He didn't remember that they were sitting on the floor of her lab, that she was his boss, he her employee. He didn't recall that he was supposed to be spying for his brothers.

Wyatt moistened his lips, dipped his head and…

Kiara uttered an impatient noise of utter irritation, slapped a palm against his chest, sprang away and scrambled to her feet. "What in the hell do you think you're doing?"

"Um, I thought I was catching you so you didn't bust your butt on the floor."

"Not that."

"What?" He got to his feet. Okay, intriguing she might be, but the woman was damn contentious.

"You were about to kiss me."

"In your dreams," he lied.

He *had* been thinking about it. No, that wasn't true. He'd done more than think about it. He'd been about to kiss her. Why had he been about to kiss her? He was skating on thin ice, borrowing trouble and a dozen other clichés that threatened to get him tossed out of Bella Notte's internship program.

Stop thinking about kissing her. Stop thinking about her as a woman. That should be easy to do. She doesn't try to attract guys—no makeup, granny clothes. Not in the least. But, hell, even the fact that she didn't try to attract him attracted him. How messed up was that? He deserved to get booted. He was acting like a hound dog.

"You licked your lips," she said.

His mind was whirling so fast that it took him a second to remember what they were talking about. "They were dry."

"And you had that look in your eye."

"Look? What look?" He tried to sound innocent but at the same time splayed a hand over his stomach. Was it pitching because of the full body contact with Kiara or because she'd read his mind?

"You know what look."

"No, honestly, I don't know what look."

"That *guy* look."

"Oh, like you're so sexy I can't control myself? Like I have to kiss you or die?" Wyatt slapped a palm over his mouth. Crap, had he actually said that out loud?

She opened her mouth, closed it. Her cheeks pinked. "I...I didn't say that."

He stepped closer. "You think it's all I can do to keep from ripping your clothes off you and making love to you?"

For the first time since he'd met her, she looked rattled, uncertain. "Forget I said anything. It was a dumb thing to say."

"Think a lot of yourself, do you?" He loved that the shoe was on the other foot and he had *her* on the run. "You think you're so tempting that you stir the animal in me?"

She backed up. "I don't think I'm tempting."

"Really?" He couldn't stop looking into those green eyes. He took another step. "Isn't that why you hide behind frumpy clothes and granny glasses? Precisely because you *are* beautiful and you're afraid your assets will get in the way of professional relationships."

"Yes...no...you're twisting my words." She was on the ropes. "I know I'm not beautiful, but I also know that men really don't need much to inspire them to lustful thoughts."

"Just because you fell on me doesn't mean you rev my engines," he lied. "You did fall on *me*."

"I told you not to steady my ladder."

"If I hadn't been there, no one would have broken your fall."

"Good." She notched her chin up. "That's the way I like it. If I fall and break myself I take full responsibility."

"You like taking full responsibility, don't you?"

"What's wrong with that?"

"You can't be fully responsible for everything. The world doesn't work that way."

"I can try."

"What are you so afraid of?"

"I'm not afraid of anything."

"No?"

"No," she said firmly.

"Why are you resistant to letting someone help you?"

"I'm not."

"You are."

"I don't like you." She took another step backward and ran into the door. She looked scared.

That wasn't good. He didn't want her to be scared of him. He couldn't ever remember a woman being scared of him. He wasn't a scary guy. Why was she scared of him?

"I don't like you," she repeated.

"Well, what do you know, we have something in common, I don't like you very much either. You're way too cranky." What was wrong with him? What had happened to the filter from his brain to his mouth? Why was he provoking her? Did he *want* to get kicked out of Bella Notte? Did he want to live down to his brothers' expectations? Was he that self-destructive? Maybe he was just defective. Aw, ouch. Raw nerve.

"You're way too glib." Her jaw hardened.

"I was simply trying to help you. If you had let me help you, none of this would have happened." He walked closer.

This time, she held her ground, balling her delicate hands in to tight little fists. "I like to do things on my own."

He clucked his tongue, covered the last step between

them until once again they were face to face. "Everyone needs help now and then."

Wyatt lowered his head.

Kiara swallowed audibly. "Not me."

"Liar," he said and then he did kiss her.

He really intended only to tease. A quick brushing of their lips to show her that kissing him wasn't such a terrible thing. But what he didn't expect was for her to sag against his chest and open her pretty mouth to him. Sweet.

Wyatt closed his eyes. She was soft and warm and pliant and, hey, maybe Steve was right after all. Maybe she was looking for an intern hook-up. She tasted tangy, like spearmint, crisp and cool, sharp and authentic. He was feeling off balance and he could have sworn he felt the earth shift.

Kiara pulled away. "Mr. Jordan," she said primly.

"Yes, Ms. Romano?" He opened his eyes.

"I don't think this relationship is going to work out in a satisfactory manner for either of us."

"Yeah?" So why she was looking at him with lust-glazed eyes?

"Yes."

"So what are you saying?"

"I'm saying, Mr. Jordan, that you're fired."

"You can't fire me. You're not paying me."

She looked taken aback. "Then I'm uninterning you. You're no longer my intern."

"Just because I caught you when you fell?"

She notched her chin up. "Yes."

"So if I'd just let you fall and break a leg, that would have been cool."

Her mouth twitched. "You're an impossible person, Mr. Jordan."

"So this whole supertaster thing, I thought you'd been searching years for my particular skill. Don't you need my tongue?" Okay, he went too far with that one, he knew it the minute he said it, but it was so much fun watching figurative steam smoke from her ears.

"Not if you were the last supertaster on the face of the earth. I'd turn to making vinegar instead. There's a ferry leaving for the mainland in three hours. Be on it."

4

Big: Wine that is very flavorful, mouth-filling.

KIARA'S MIND WAS in turmoil. She couldn't believe Wyatt Jordan's sheer audacity. She spent her days in a lab or in the vineyard. She was unaccustomed to men like him, charming cads who didn't take no for an answer, brash fellows who called her on her opinions, sexy guys who heated her up from the inside out with one sizzling glance.

It unnerved her. Irritated her. Scared her.

And when Kiara got scared, she got tough.

"Just like that?" Wyatt murmured. "No second chances?" He shot her a hangdog look.

No more strays. One black kitty was enough.

"Look, Mr. Jordan, I run a tight ship. It has to be this way. This winery supports my entire family. The quality of our product rests on my shoulders. I can't have some glib guy making a joke of my livelihood."

"I wasn't making a joke."

"Be that as it may, I simply don't think you're Bella Notte intern material."

"There's nothing I can do to convince you otherwise?"

"No—" Kiara only got out one word before a sharp jolting sensation rocked the earth, interrupting her. A stronger version of the faint tremor she'd felt on the ladder. Felt and had assumed was her own weak-kneed silliness over Wyatt.

Beakers rattled. Pipettes rolled over the counter, crashed to the floor, scattering splinters of glass. The ground shook, trembling for several long seconds that felt more like hours.

Kiara and Wyatt lurched into each other. He slipped an arm around her waist. She didn't protest. She was too stunned. She should have drawn back. She would have drawn back except his warm touch instantly soothed and oriented her dizzy head.

They stared into each other's eyes and simultaneously breathed. "Earthquake."

"At least a five-pointer," Wyatt said.

"Probably a six." Kiara pulled away from him and placed a hand to the wall to steady herself against the faint tremors still vibrating through the ground.

"You're bleeding," he said.

Her gaze rested on his face. Her breath stilled in her lungs.

His smile, quick and ready, sent her head reeling.

"Kiara," he repeated, her name coming out low and husky in the quiet room. "You're bleeding."

"What?" She startled, glanced down, acknowledging now, a sliver of flying glass had embedded in the pad of her thumb. "Oh."

"Let me." Wyatt said, reaching for a tissue from the box that had fallen on the floor. Before she could protest, he took her hand in his warm palm, hooked his fingers around her wrist and with his other hand, wrapped the tissue around the shard and deftly removed it.

Fresh blood bloomed. He dabbed it with the corner of the other end of the tissue until the bleeding stopped.

Kiara stood there, acutely aware of the heat and scent of this man invading her personal space, but she did not feel threatened. In fact, his proximity made her feel strangely safe.

He looked her in the eyes, then lowered his head, raised their joined hands and gently kissed the pad of her wounded thumb.

It was the simplest kiss in the world. Light, tender and over so quickly she wasn't sure he'd done it.

For a moment, she stared at him, thumb tingling from his touch, transfixed.

From outside the lab came the sounds of people spilling from the buildings, chattering in excited tones. There were guests on the premises. She had to make sure everyone was okay and she had to put some distance between herself and Wyatt.

"I have to go check on things."

"I'll go with you." Wyatt was already heading for the door.

She wanted to tell him no, to just leave, but he was already leading the way from the lab, opening the side door and then standing aside for her to exit.

His dark eyes gleamed as if he were enjoying himself. What was that all about? An earthquake turned him on? Some people got an adrenaline high from natural phenomena like tornadoes and earthquakes. Was he one of them?

Maybe it's not the earthquake that turned him on.

Kiara shoved that thought aside. She didn't have time for Wyatt Jordan and the strange, unwanted attraction she felt for him.

The first person she saw was her Grandfather Romano. His shock of thick white hair was mussed, but he did not look alarmed. He'd come from the visitor center with a trail of bug-eyed tourists following behind him.

"It was not such a big one," he said. "A few broken bottles. Some cracks in the walls. Not like the quake of '89. We lost half our vineyard in that one."

"Felt pretty big to me," mumbled a pale elderly woman leaning heavily on a cane.

"How can these people live in a place where the earth shakes willy-nilly?" asked her companion.

"We live here," Grandfather Romano said, sweeping his hand grandly, "because there is no more beautiful place on earth to grow grapes."

"There's Napa," Wyatt said to Kiara.

Kiara snorted. "Idyll is far superior to Napa."

"According to the Romanos."

"You like Napa so much, go intern there."

At that moment, Maurice appeared from the main house, his wife Trudy coming up behind him. "We'll round up the interns, enlist their help inspecting the vineyards," he said.

"I'll check out the refrigeration unit," Kiara offered. "Grandfather, please take our guests into the tasting room. Have Grandmamma put out a cheese tray and open some wine. Free samples for everyone."

A cheer went up from the crowd.

The earthquake wasn't her fault, but the guests would remember how she'd turned their negative experience into a positive one. Yes, it would cost some money, but good PR went a long way, especially when the bulk of their profits came from onsite sales.

Kiara strode across the well-landscaped grounds, alert and searching for signs of damage. Wyatt kept up with her, stride for stride. The guy was about as easy to get rid of as bedbugs, but what surprised her was the warm rush of gratitude that winnowed through her. It felt nice, having someone at her side.

Are you freaking kidding me? Nice? Since when have you ever needed nice?

Right. What was she thinking? She'd just fired the guy for being too forward. Kiara grimaced.

The minute they stepped into the refrigeration room it became immediately clear that something was amiss. A horrible rattling noise was coming from one of the machines.

"Oh, dear." Kiara rushed forward.

"Sounds like the compressor," Wyatt said.

Kiara groaned. "That's going to be expensive."

Wyatt stepped to the back of the unit, bent over and inspected the undercarriage. She shouldn't have been staring at his butt. She had far more important things to be thinking about, but she couldn't seem to stop her gaze from tracking up the length of his long legs to where his backside was cradled snugly in his jeans.

Enchanted, Kiara caught her bottom lip up between her teeth. She was so focused on his gorgeous ass that when her cell phone vibrated in her pocket, she jumped.

Wyatt raised his head. "You okay?"

"My phone." She pulled the cell phone from the pocket of her apron.

Wyatt went back to inspecting the refrigeration unit.

"Hello," she said into the phone, her gaze still trained on Wyatt. There ought to be a law against looking so damned sexy.

"Kiara, it's your mother."

"Did you feel the quake in the city?"

"We did. It was a little unsettling. Flashbacks to 1989." Her mother chuckled. "But really not that bad. We heard on the news that there were some minor mishaps. Nothing major. How's Bella Notte?"

Kiara cast a glance at the refrigeration unit. She didn't want to upset her parents. They were in San Francisco for her father's checkup following a rigorous course of chemotherapy. Besides, this was nothing. A minor blip in the grand scheme of things.

"Great," she said. "Hardly worth noting. How's Dad?"

"He got a clean bill of health." Her mother's voice was heavy with relief. "The PET scan showed no reoccurrence of the cancer."

Kiara let out a deep breath, only just then realizing she'd been holding it. "Mom, that's so great."

"It is good news. But, we're stuck here for another night at least. The earthquake did some minor damage to the ferry dock and there'll be no ferries to or from the island until they get it repaired. They seemed optimistic that it will be operational by no later than the day after tomorrow."

"We'll see you when we see you. Everything is fine here so don't worry."

"You're such a good daughter," her mother said. "I never have to worry about you like I do your sister."

"Deidre's still young, Mom. Give her some time to figure things out." Kiara's younger sister had dropped out of college to sing in a band. She lived hand to mouth, traveling all over the country, bunking with whoever had a ready couch, getting into various minor scrapes along the way.

"You didn't need to figure things out."

"She's a free-spirit." Something Kiara had never wanted to be. She had been born responsible and a bit of a control freak. She insisted on shouldering more than her share of the burden at Bella Notte, although her family kept trying to get her to relax, slow down, take a vacation. She just wasn't built that way, but that didn't mean she couldn't understand her younger sister's need for adventure. Kiara had never had such an urge. She was happy here. She knew who she was and what she wanted out of life. She'd never needed to figure it out. "Dee just needs time and space to grow into herself."

Dee had come home when their father had first been diagnosed, but during his bout with chemo, she'd said she couldn't deal with seeing him suffer and she'd taken off again. Maybe Kiara should have judged her sister for it, but the truth was, she'd taken on more and more of the daily operations of Bella Notte as her way of coping with her father's illness. It was easier to work hard, keep her mind busy so she didn't have to think about losing him.

"I hope you're right."

"Stop worrying. Enjoy Dad's good news. Go out and celebrate."

"You're right," her mother said. "I'll call you when we're on our way home."

"I'll let Grandfather and Grandmamma know. Goodbye." She ended the call.

"Kiara?" In Wyatt's deep-throated voice her name sounded like a one-word poem.

A sweet shiver ran through her.

She turned to find him on his back on the floor, peering up at the bottom of the refrigeration unit. "Yes?" she kept her tone steady.

"It might be something fairly simple like the fan blade."

Kiara pressed her palms together in a silent prayer. Please let it be something simple like the fan blade. She was barely making payroll as it was and in order to be able to afford insurance, they had been forced to take out a policy with a huge deductible. Granted, insurance would cover some of the damage they'd experienced, but certainly not all of it. Plus, with the ferries being out of commission, by the time a repairman got over to the island the wine could spoil. Anything Wyatt could do to save her time and money would be a godsend.

"I think I can fix it," he ventured.

"You're a refrigeration repairman?"

"Not exactly."

"Why should I trust you to fix it? You're just trying to keep your job. I'll call someone to come out."

"From the mainland?"

Shoot.

The unit had to be repaired, but the repair service they used was in San Francisco. From what her mother had said about the ferry landing, no one was getting in or out by water for at least a day or two.

"If you've got a tool kit, I can fix this," Wyatt promised.

She didn't want to rely on him, but what choice did she have? Maurice was hopeless at anything mechanical and grandfather had cataracts. He'd have a difficult time seeing the fan motor, much less repairing it. Her dad was the one who usually made the simple repairs around the vineyard. Or he used to before he'd gotten cancer. She should have already hired a part-time maintenance man, but she'd been trying to save money.

Wyatt pushed up off the floor and got to his feet, dusting his hands against the seat of his faded blue jeans. "Tell me where the tools are and I'll get right to work."

Against her better judgment, Kiara showed him to the tool shed. She entered ahead of Wyatt, flipping on the lights. The interior was hot and crowded with tools, supplies and equipment. Perspiration beaded on the nape of her neck and corresponding beads of sweat pearled on Wyatt's forehead. He started grabbing tools.

"Do you need a tool belt?" she asked.

"It would help."

She snatched a leather tool belt from the shelf and tossed it to Wyatt. He strapped the leather holster around his lean waist. He filled the pockets with a hammer, a drill, screwdrivers, a soldering iron.

Kiara stared at him, taken aback by how different he seemed with a tool belt on him. Now, he appeared competent, capable, far less flippant.

But was he really able to repair her unit or was he just showing off because he wanted her to reconsider her decision to kick him out? If he fixed it, in all fairness, she *should* reconsider her decision. Especially since most of it was predicated on the fact that the attraction she felt for him affected her to the core.

"You're certain you can do this?" She narrowed her eyes. "You're not yanking my chain?"

"Oh, ye of little faith."

"Your hands look kind of soft. Not vineyard hands at all."

"I'm tougher than I look." There was a sudden edge to his voice that matched the sharpened expression on his face.

Kiara didn't want to be captivated, but the man looked impossibly compelling with the tools strapped to his waist, testosterone oozing from him. She felt trapped in a dreamy bubble of pure sensation where every touch, every action was weighted with sexual tension.

Wyatt shoved a hand through the thick lock of hair that had fallen over his forehead. Mesmerized, Kiara followed his movements. Followed him like a puppy when he went back to the refrigeration room.

Wyatt assumed his spot on the cement floor once more.

Kiara paced, arms akimbo, and prayed Wyatt could fix it. Her gaze tracked to Wyatt's legs. "How's it going?"

"Could you give me some space to work?" Wyatt asked. "It's hard to concentrate with you breathing down my neck."

"Okay, I'll just go stand over here." Kiara walked to the opposite side of the room. "Go on."

Wyatt shot her a go-away look, but went back to what he was doing. A couple of minutes later he let out a curse.

"What's wrong? What is it? Did you break something?"

"It's nothing. I curse a lot when I'm working. It's a guy thing."

"Can I help? Do you want me to hold your flashlight?"

Grinning, Wyatt sat up, crossed his legs tailor-style.

It was only then that Kiara realized how that last comment sounded and felt her cheeks burn. Thankfully, he did not volley back with some suggestive retort.

"I was thinking outside might be a better place for you. I'm sure there's a hundred other things you need to check on," he said.

"You mean go off and leave you alone in here?"

He nodded, widened his eyes comically. "Uh-huh, just like that."

"But I don't even know you. What if you were sent here by my competition to sabotage my winery?"

"You do know how paranoid that sounds, right? It's not like I orchestrated the earthquake."

He was right. She did sound paranoid. "Scratch that, I know you're not here to sabotage my winery. I'm just—"

"A bit of a control freak."

"I wouldn't say *freak*."

"Control Nazi?"

"All right, I get the picture. You want to be left alone to work in peace."

"No offense."

"None taken."

Wyatt went back to banging his tools.

Feeling dismissed, Kiara wondered how she'd lost control of the situation. Wyatt was right. She felt insecure when she wasn't on top of everything and she really didn't want to leave him alone. For all she knew he could cause more damage to the refrigeration unit.

But honestly, there were other things she should be doing. It wasn't easy for her, but she was simply going to have to trust him.

THE SECOND KIARA left the room, Wyatt got to his feet, snagged the cell phone from his pocket and put in an emergency call to his brothers.

"'Lo," Eric said, answering on the first ring.

"I'm here. At Bella Notte."

"You feel the quake out there? News is saying it was 5.9."

"Yeah." Wyatt thought of Kiara's lips and her smoky-green eyes. "I felt the quake. It's why I'm calling."

"Look at you, baby brother. All James Bond and stuff."

"Hardly James Bond."

"Problems?"

"Kiara Romano took an instant disliking to me."

"You?" Eric hooted. "Unable to charm a woman? What? Doesn't she like men?"

"No." Wyatt scratched his head. "I definitely don't get that vibe. I think I rub her the wrong way."

"You better get rubbing her the right way. I got the new sales figures and we're down two percent in dessert reds, but guess whose sales are up?"

"Bella Notte."

"You got it. I still can't believe Kiara's not drooling over your pretty bod. Will miracles never cease? I didn't know there was a straight woman on the planet who wouldn't fall at your feet."

"Ha, ha. I've met my match. Yada, yada. Can we move on?"

"So are you going to be able to stay there if she dislikes you so much?"

"That's just it, she's already kicked me off the island."

"C'mon, Wyatt." Eric grunted. "Take her down. She's one woman running a tiny little winery."

Making damn fine wine. Wyatt heard the disappointment in his brother's voice vibrating through the airwaves, felt it twist his gut. Dammit, if he hadn't outgrown the need to impress his older siblings…

"I thought you wanted to prove to Scott and me that you'd grown up. So do it."

"All is not lost, thanks to the earthquake."

"How's that?"

"The quake caused some minor damage to their refrigeration unit. At least I hope it's minor."

"No, no, damage is good. We need to crush Bella Notte before they ever have a chance to rise up off the mat. No holds barred, bro." His brother was always ready with a wrestling metaphor. Eric had taken the Princeton wrestling team to the championship during his reign. Wyatt made it a point never to wrestle Eric. He always lost.

"Repairing the damage is a way of me keeping the job. Besides, if I don't do it, she'll just find someone else who will."

"Let me get this straight." Eric chortled. "*You're* going to repair a refrigerator unit?"

"Laugh it up, fuzzball."

"Beyond unhooking a woman's bra in under ten seconds, you have no mechanical skills whatsoever."

"I have *more* skills than you think. I own a yacht."

"That a mechanic fixes when it's necessary."

"I've done some repairs myself."

"So what do you need me for? I can't fix a refrigeration unit."

"Duly noted. Just connect me to the head of our maintenance department."

"That I can do. Hang on."

A few minutes later he was talking to the head of De-Salme's winery-maintenance department and the guy was talking him through repairing Kiara's refrigeration unit. Luckily, as Wyatt had suspected, it turned out to be nothing more than the condenser fan that had been warped by bumping up against the coils during the vibration of the earthquake. All he had to do was disassemble the condenser, hammer out the bent fan blade and put it back together.

He'd no sooner hung up with the refrigeration guru and tightened the last screw holding the fan in place when Kiara entered the room.

"How's it going?" she asked.

Wyatt got to his feet, holstered his screwdriver and dusted off his palms. The unit hummed quietly. "Finished."

Kiara looked impressed and incredulous. "You pulled it off?"

His instinct was to gloat, but instead he shrugged. "All in a day's work."

"I can't believe you did it."

"Your confidence in me is overwhelming."

"Thank you," she said.

"So does this mean I get my second chance?" He lowered his voice and his eyelids, studying her closely.

"I suppose I'm obligated." She stuffed her hands into

the pockets of her apron, rotating her shoulders forward in a gesture that closed her in, shut him out.

Wyatt might not be an expert on condenser fans, but he knew women. "Something else is bothering you," he murmured. "Can I help?"

She waved a hand, nodded. "No."

"You're sending mixed messages."

"What?"

"You nodded but said no. My experience has taught me that body language speaks louder than words."

"Who are you exactly?"

"I'm just a guy who's interested in making wine."

"What do you do for a living? Most of our interns are students. You're too old for that."

"I do a little PR work now and again."

"When you're not being a slacker or repairing condenser fans?"

"That's right."

She cocked her head. "I can see that. Cut the hair, shave the beard, I'm sure you look very slick."

"Sarcasm?"

"Truth."

He stepped closer. "Why don't you like me?"

"You seem to like yourself well enough for the both of us. I wouldn't worry about whether I like you or not."

"You make a good point."

She shifted from one foot to the other. "I'm being tacky, aren't I? I apologize. It's been an…unexpected day."

"Honestly, if there's something else I can help with I'd be happy to jump in."

Kiara gave him a look he couldn't identify. "Does that usually work well for you?"

"What?" He feigned innocence.

"That genuine insincerity."

"I'm not insincere," he protested.

"Just very PR."

"I do have a way with women." He couldn't help grinning.

"And modest too." She snorted, folded her arms over her chest. "What a catch."

"You really *don't* like me, do you?"

Kiara shrugged. "You're growing on me. Sort of like mold."

He laughed. "Good mold, like penicillin?"

"That remains to be seen."

"You are such a skeptic."

"Scientist," she corrected. "I'm a scientist. We're taught to dig deep, skim far below the surface."

"And what do you see when you look at me?" He didn't know why he was inviting her critique. It was bound to be harsh. Wyatt had never been a glutton for punishment. Why now?

"As champion of living life on the surface."

5

Bead: A poetic metaphor for the bubbles in a sparkling wine.

FOR THE REMAINDER of that day, Wyatt and the other interns worked with the entire crew of Bella Notte, including Mia, Samual, Elliott and Juliet, to clean up after the earthquake. Kiara avoided Wyatt as much as she could, spending most of her time tallying the damage and talking to friends and neighbors in town. By and large, most everyone reported only minor injuries and minimal damage. The earthquake had been startlingly inconvenient, but no long-term problems for Idyll. By midnight, they squared away the majority of the mess and everyone fell into bed exhausted.

The following morning, Wyatt arrived at the lab at 7:00 a.m. on the dot, smirkless and ready to work. He was dressed in a pair of olive-green cargo shorts that hit him just above the knee and a white-and-maroon Bella Notte polo shirt. He'd combed his hair and shaved his beard stubble. He smelled of sandalwood soap and ocean breezes and he seemed to be taking his second chance seriously. The fact that he was trying to reform went a long way to earning Kiara's forgiveness.

Unwise, unwise, whispered her subconscious mind. Especially after the restless night she'd spent, tossing and turning, sleeping in fits and starts. Battling sizzling hot-sex dreams where a shirtless Wyatt was the star attraction. Remembering the heat of his fevered touch in the darkness of her fantasy pushed Kiara's thoughts to the edge.

It was daylight, she reminded herself. She was a grown-up. She could handle working with him.

"I'm ready," Wyatt said mildly. "Tell me what you need done."

"I'm putting your nose into service."

"Sounds painful," he teased.

"Do you know what *Brettanomyces* is?"

"It's a yeast that commonly causes spoilage in the production of red wine."

Surprised by his knowledge, Kiara threw him a sidelong look. "That's correct."

"What? You think I'm just a pretty face?" he joked.

"Most particularly Brett attacks sweet reds like Decadent Midnight," she went on, doing her best to ignore his tease. "To help control it, I rigorously work the vineyards to achieve fruit maturity at lower levels of alcohol, but Brett is still an issue."

"Where do I come in?"

"Brett smells like a sweaty saddle and if it gets in the wine, it makes it taste like that."

"Not the flavor we're shooting for."

"No, and the equipment for detecting and dealing with Brett is extremely expensive. We could saturate the wine with sulfur dioxide and then strongly filtrate it, but that affects the taste. The key is to keep Brett out of the wine to begin with."

"So, you want me to sniff your grapes?"

"In a word," she said, "yes. But first we're going to the wine cellar and I'm going to let you sample a bottle of wine that I believe has gone Bretty."

"Horse sweat, yum, can't wait."

"It won't be that bad. If it's Bretty, it's only marginally so, which is why I'm having you taste it. Anyone can spot a heavily Bretty wine, but it takes a discerning tongue to pick it up in minute levels."

"I'm game. Let's go." He looked at her with shrewd eyes, as if he knew exactly how she'd spent her turbulent night.

Kiara gulped, felt her cheeks heat.

He moved toward the door and even through the chemical lab smells, his scent wafted her way, that fresh masculine scent that had haunted her dreams.

Kiara took off ahead of him, striding for the wine cellar via the exit at the side of the house, rather than going down the corridor inside the house with him.

In the 1970s her grandfather had put in the extra door so they could take tourists into the cellar without having to lead them through the family's main residence. She needed a dose of fresh air before getting into the confines of the cellar with him. Needed to clear her head of sticky, unwanted thoughts, like, how good he smelled and how cute he looked without the scraggly beard. Take away the glasses and he'd be a knockout.

Why had she suggested going to the cellar? She'd just made up some job for him because once she'd peered into those mesmerizing brown eyes, she couldn't remember what she had planned for that day. This was crazy, the way he robbed her mind of all rational thought.

"Hey." Wyatt sprinted after her. "Wait up."

She forced herself to slow down and let him catch up. She didn't want to slow down but running off and leaving him felt as if she was losing control again.

You are *losing control. Snap out of it. Do whatever you have to in order to fend off this…this…*

This what?

"Do you always walk like you're on your way to put out a fire?" he asked.

"I'm not a leisurely person. I don't do anything slowly."

"Nothing?" he drawled, his tone full of innuendo.

"Nothing."

"That's a shame."

"What's a shame?"

"That you don't know how to slow down."

"Slow is for slackers," she retorted.

"Touché," he said, "but slacking can be fun."

"I don't do fun," she said. "Fun is a waste of time. Fun is what causes trouble."

"Trouble? How does fun cause trouble?"

"Idle hands…" she began.

"Enjoy themselves," he finished.

Kiara frowned. "Life isn't about enjoyment."

"No?" He sounded as if he were trying not to laugh at her. "What's it about?"

What was so funny? "No. It's about hard work and sacrifice and doing the right thing."

"Hmm, doesn't sound like my kind of life."

"Well, it's the life of a winery owner and if you don't

want to work hard, then you don't belong in the wine-making business."

"And yet, the product you make is all about relaxing and having fun. Isn't that contradictory?"

"Life is full of paradoxes."

"I don't think that's it at all," he said.

She paused with her hand on the combination lock of the door that led to the cellar and turned to glance at him. "You know what? It really doesn't matter what you think."

"No?" He sounded as if he was struggling not to laugh.

"No."

He grinned at her, sunlight dappling through the leaves of the cottonwood tree planted next to the house. "Chicken."

Her pulse skittered at the challenge in his eyes. She dialed in the combination to the lock and yanked open the cellar door. She rushed down the steps only to stop at the bottom when she saw that Maurice was showing a group of tourists around.

Kiara backed away, hooked her hand around Wyatt's elbow and pulled him up the steps with her and into the sunlight. "It's too crowded down there. Let's wait for them to finish," she said, feeling oddly breathless.

He nodded, and seemed breathless too. She wondered if he felt as overwhelmed and off-kilter as she did. Maybe giving him a second chance had been a big mistake.

She realized then that she was still holding on to his elbow. She inhaled sharply, the sound a harsh rasp in the clear morning air. Hand trembling, she let go of him and moved to one side. They stood there a long moment, saying nothing to each other and then, in hesitant increments, her gaze shifted to meet his and time spun out endlessly between them.

Wyatt's gaze stabbed hers.

She saw it in his eyes, the same wanting that was eating her up inside.

The door opened and Maurice appeared, herding the group of tourists out with him. Relief spread through Kiara. Ducking her head, she plunged down the steps to the safety of the cellar, her favorite place in the winery besides the lab.

Except, the minute the door closed behind Wyatt it occurred to her that she was now trapped down here alone with him—alone in the wine cellar, alone with the sweet smell of wine and seductive lighting and the hungry taste of lust.

He sauntered toward her in the musky dimness. Romantic Romano relatives had placed strategic recessed lighting in the ceiling to produce a cozy, dreamy atmosphere. It worked too well.

Wyatt stood with the indolent, loose-limbed sprawl of a man fully comfortable in his own skin. He had one arm slung over the edge of shelving, the crook of his elbow caught around the aged wooden bracket as if he were about to edge the structure out onto a dance floor. He cut an intriguing figure—tall, dark-haired, mysterious. His dangerous, full-lipped smile said, *c'mon let's play.*

Kiara was pragmatic, sober, not given to flights of fancy, but in that moment, in this lighting, her imagination overtook her sensible nature.

His eyes, as languid and warm as the summer sun, landed on hers.

Immediately, she lowered her eyelids, acutely aware of her sudden labored breathing and the heated awareness warming her skin. She felt a rush, a push, a thrust of energy that curled inside her, both heavy and light. She couldn't help glancing at him again.

His gaze roved over her in a mesmerized inspection, making her feel completely naked. She raised a hand to her throat. His gaze returned to her face, hung on her lips.

"Aren't you going to offer me a taste of that Bretty wine?" he murmured, his soft smile causing her body to spark with a jumble of sensations, all of them disturbingly good. "Isn't that what we came down here for?"

Was it? She couldn't even remember.

Enchanted, she stared into the dark center of his eyes and she was lost to the insanity that had taken hold of her since the moment Wyatt had arrived at Bella Notte. She hauled in a deep breath.

He did the same.

That's when she understood he was feeling as overcome and off-balance as she, and he was wielding that cocky grin as a shield to hide his vulnerability. They studied each other in dual wonder. It seemed neither of them knew what to make of this surging chemistry.

"Kiara?" he whispered.

She licked her lips. "Um…yes, yes, the wine."

Turning, she moved deeper into the cellar where the older wines were kept, some from as far back as when her great-grandfather had started the winery after prohibition. She felt Wyatt coming behind her through the catacombs of shelving and gleaming wine bottles, his big body taking up too much space.

What was this? How could she be so befuddled over

a total stranger? She always kept her emotions carefully wrapped up, a defense against her family's romanticism, a way to preserve her common sense. It took her a long time to make friends, even longer to trust someone intimately. Keeping her feelings in check kept her safe and sensible. It was the one thing that differentiated her from all the other Romanos. She prized her self-control and here it was, *poof,* gone. This thing—whatever it was—pledged a big thrill, yet at the same time promised serious trouble.

She stopped at the very back of the cellar and plucked a bottle of a red dessert wine, a generational precursor to Decadent Midnight, from the rack, the familiar heft of it a comfort in her hand, and then tugged a corkscrew from her apron pocket.

"May I?" Wyatt asked, extending his hand.

She was cornered between his body and the back wall of the cellar. No way out.

Reluctantly, she passed him the bottle and the corkscrew. In the hand off, their fingers brushed.

Kiara inhaled audibly. Slowly, she raised her head and met his stare. Time stretched into infinity.

She'd never experienced anything quite like this before. Because her family depended on her, because she was so absorbed in the science of winemaking, she'd always avoided serious romantic entanglements.

But this feeling, which clearly promised to turn her world upside-down, not only scared her, it excited her. What was wrong with her? She should just fire him again and be done with it.

Wyatt opened the wine, set the corkscrew on the shelf. "Do you have a glass?"

"Just drink from the bottle," she said. "It's not good wine. You won't want more than a swallow."

His dark-eyed gaze landed on hers and he took a sip, studying her down the long, smooth length of the bottle. He held the wine in his mouth for a long moment before he swallowed it down.

"You're right," he said, "it's very faint, but the undertones are dark, heavy."

"It could just be a case of earthy terroir," she said.

"It's Brett," he confirmed, "but then some people might be willing to accept a dark taste in exchange for an organic wine."

The complexity of his palate stunned her. "You can tell it's organic?"

"It goes with the territory. Brett is not dangerous yeast and it's quite common in organic vineyards. It simply becomes a matter of taste."

"Being a die-hard romantic, my great-grandfather believed in organic cultivation, but he had a difficult time keeping his wine tasty because of all the bacteria and bugs in organic wine. Later, Grandfather tried to keep up the family tradition, but as Bella Notte struggled to make a superior wine, he reluctantly turned to using scientific methods of grape cultivation. It saved our winery."

"But now," Wyatt said, "the cultural climate is changing, organic products are big again and there's a backlash against science interfering with nature."

"Yes. I want to supply my customer base with the products they want without eschewing science. It's a delicate balance. One I've yet to strike."

He leaned closer. "In school, you learned a reductionist approach."

"How do you know that?" She marveled at his understanding. He knew far more about wine than he'd initially let on.

"Because it's the nature of science. To reduce things down to their individual components and focus on each element separately, but there are limits to reductionism. This day and age it's smart to have a holistic approach to winemaking. But you're conflicted about that too. On the one hand, there's your logical, scientific mind that likes putting things into boxes. But on the other hand, there's your innate knowing—the instinctual part of you that you fight to deny that knows the truth. Face it, Kiara, there are some things in life that just can't be quantified or qualified."

"That paradox again," she muttered, surprised at how well he seemed to know her. Was she that easy to read? Or was he simply that intuitive?

"You have a hard time admitting that science cannot control everything, that some things are just…magic," he said, his voice husky and she knew he was no longer talking about wine.

"I don't believe in magic."

"But you want to."

Yes, yes, she wanted to believe. She wanted to let herself go, get swept away, be imaginative and spontaneous and romantic like the rest of her family. She wanted to succumb to the madness.

This rampaging urge to kiss Wyatt—oh, who was she kidding—to have sex with him, spoke to her as nothing ever had. Her hormones had never ruled her. In all honesty, that's why she'd fired him, because he unraveled her in nine-hundred startling ways.

As if arranged, they moved toward each other. In

perfect unison, his hands moved to remove her glasses while she reached to pluck the glasses from his face. With his frames dangling from her fingers, and her frames dangling from his, she wrapped her arms around his neck.

Wyatt pulled her close, kissed her hard.

His kiss set her ablaze, triggered emotional turmoil, stunned her. What was this? How could she— headstrong, business-minded Kiara feel so befuddled by feminine passion?

Go, go, urged her body.

No, no, scolded her mind.

She deepened the kiss, introducing *her* tongue to his. Yesterday's kiss had opened Pandora's box and she could not close it back. He tasted big. Robust. Rockingly righteous. Better than Decadent Midnight.

Oh, crap. What are you doing? Are you insane?

Insanity. Yes. That's what this was. Some kind of temporary hormonal insanity. It would pass. It had to pass.

He tasted raw and real, but her heart, the stupid heart she'd tried so hard to deny, overflowed with mushy thoughts like—heavenly, magical, electric.

Their mouths mated. Hotly. Wildly. Kiara remember her first ride on the Tilt-a-Whirl. *This* was a hundred times more dizzying. With the Tilt-a-Whirl you knew the ride would eventually end if you just held on long enough. Would that strategy work here as well?

Battle it. Don't give in. Fight, fight.

Kiara yanked away, dragged in a breath. Extended his glasses to him with a quivering hand.

His hair was mussed. His eyes glazed. He looked… *thunderstruck.*

This wasn't her. She didn't do things like this. She never allowed her desires to overrun her common sense.

Well, it's happening now.

He took both their glasses, stuck them on the shelf with the corkscrew and wine bottle, and then kissed her again.

Yes, she was weak and foolish and…and…

It felt so good. *He* felt so good.

Making love to Wyatt would mark her in ways she couldn't imagine. She knew that she would be forever changed. There would be no going back. No undoing this. She understood that. And yet, even though she knew he was a huge risk, she couldn't stop craving him.

She was running on pure emotion and her logical brain barely paused. She felt giddy, out of control, reckless, forbidden. And she wanted him with an all-consuming need.

Kiara surrendered. When he pulled her closer, she did not resist. In fact, stepped happily into his embrace. A bubble of joy beaded up through her, fizzy as champagne, ambushed her. A heady sense of ultimate rightness settled over her, as if by being with him she was finally set free from herself.

His hands went to her shoulders, and he looked deeply into her eyes.

"Kiara," he breathed.

Her anxious fingers worried the collar of his polo shirt, her eyes held prisoner by his. She was his captive and nothing had ever felt so sweet. In her hands she fisted the hem of his shirt, and began to slowly roll it up the length of his lean, muscled torso.

How odd, but how wonderful it felt to stand here in

the circle of his arms. What could she have if she was willing to let go of control? To trust a little?

He helped her wrestle the shirt over his head. His skin was tanned and dotted with curly black hair. Her fingers skimmed over the honed ridges of his muscles, the pale light a sharp contrast to his sun-burnished color. He was Hollywood handsome. She was a lab geek. A cork dork. An introverted nerd of the highest order. What did a man like him see in a woman like her?

The answer didn't matter, at least not now. All that mattered at this moment was the hot, desperate need speeding through her body and escaping from her lungs on a soft sigh. "You look drinkable."

"Have a taste," he invited.

She chuckled. "You smell good too. Not Bretty at all."

Wyatt's eyes lit up and a smile carved his face. "Good enough to eat?"

"Yum." And then she did the brashest thing she had ever done in her life. She licked him.

His hearty laugh rang out to roll around the room. His delight delighted her. The sound vibrated up through his chest and into her palms and she caught his joy. "How do I taste?"

"Salty," she pronounced.

"You, Kiara Romano, are a surprise. I suspected as much all along."

"What do you mean?"

"You're far more romantic than you want to admit."

"I suppose you're an expert on romance?"

"I wouldn't say expert…" He trailed off.

"Ever been married?"

"Nope."

"Have you ever been close?"

"Never."

"Why not?"

"I could ask you the same question."

"How do you know I haven't been?"

"I asked around."

She was both pleased and annoyed to learn that he had been asking questions about her. She was tempted to ask him what else he'd discovered about her, but he dipped his head and claimed her lips.

Wyatt swallowed the soft sound of pleasure that escaped her throat. His lips intoxicated her as surely as if she'd downed an entire bottle of Decadent Midnight.

His mouth teased, playful and daring. Tempting her to follow him down a road it might be smarter not to tread. His tongue coaxed, cajoled, seduced.

Oh, the promises his kisses suggested, of pleasures she'd never even dared dream. Kiara kissed him back, as fully engaged as he, pressed her body against his, the material of her cotton dress rubbing against his bare chest.

One hand drifted boldly to his belt buckle.

"Kiara," he whispered. "Are you sure you want to start this?"

No, no, she wasn't sure. Not sure at all. She knew it was a dumb thing to do—an affair with an intern. Dumb on so many levels and yet, she simply did not care. That shocked her. But instead of answering, she slid her arms around his neck and tugged his head down for more kisses.

He reached for the buttons at the front of her dress, his fingers easing them open as he continued to kiss her.

She was so caught up in the tender thrust of his tongue that she almost didn't hear her cell phone buzz.

"You've got a call," he said in a pensive voice.

Kiara fished it from her pocket and saw Maurice's name on the caller ID. She switched it over to voice mail and then set her phone on the wine rack beside the corkscrew, the bottle of Bretty wine and their eyeglasses.

"Problem solved," she said.

Wyatt looked at her incredulously. "You're not going to get that?"

"You know what? I'm tired of being on call 24/7, 365 days a year. Let someone else field the problems for once. Whatever it is can wait."

The second the words were out of her mouth, Kiara stood stunned unable to believe she'd uttered them. She was always available for the family. Night or day. Another time, with any other person, she would have answered Maurice. Part of her felt guilty. After all, her cousin needed her. It could very well be important. But guilt faded to nothingness in the face of the very real, very raw desire thundering through her.

Wyatt made her feel things she'd never felt before. Made her want things she'd never wanted. Maybe she never knew just how much she was at the beck and call of everyone in her family. Her life wasn't her own, but until now, that had never bothered her.

What was he doing to her? Who was she becoming?

Before she had a chance to answer those questions, Wyatt's mouth was nibbling at her neck. Kiara tossed her head, giving him full access to her throat. The feel of his tender lips at her pulse unraveled a burning heat deep within her feminine core. The pull was irresistible and she relaxed into it, succumbing to Wyatt's masculinity. She'd never been an overtly sexual woman, but around him, everything was different.

She was different.

His fingers finished unbuttoning her dress and he eased it down the length of her body. A soft sigh unfurled her lips as he edged the fabric over her hips.

A gentle tug sent the garment plunging to her feet, leaving her standing in front of Wyatt in her sensible sports bra and white cotton boy-cut panties and her hiking shoes. She should have felt vulnerable, exposed, embarrassed, but she didn't.

What she couldn't figure out was why he was staring at her as if she was the sexiest thing he'd ever laid eyes on.

Wyatt splayed his palms across the cheeks of her butt and leaned into her as he guided them both downward onto the rammed-earth floor. His mouth swept maddeningly slow kisses over the hollow of her throat to the top of her breasts. His fingers worked at the clasp of her bra and shortly, he banished the underwear to some far reaches of the wine cellar.

He cradled her in his arms and kissed her belly while one hand untied the laces of her hiking boots and slipped them off her feet, first one and then the other. Then he methodically disposed of her socks. Her bare toes curled against the warm earth.

"You are so beautiful," Wyatt pronounced, pulling back to look at her with appreciative eyes.

For the first time, she felt self-conscious. She wasn't beautiful and she knew it. She didn't even try to make herself beautiful like most women did. She rarely bothered with makeup and took no notice of her clothes. Her nails were ravaged by work and the only jewelry she wore was her simple gold stud earrings. She put on what was comfortable in the offices, the lab and the vineyards.

"You're so real and honest," he murmured. "There's nothing artificial about you." He ran a hand down her legs. They were toned from daily walks through the vineyards. His hand settled at the waist of her panties. It was her last barrier on the road to complete surrender.

She quivered, tense with anticipation.

"Wyatt." She gasped. "I need you."

"I need you too," he said gruffly.

He stood and she rose to her knees, her eager fingers yanking at his belt, fumbling for his zipper.

"Wait," he said, dug a condom from his wallet and fisted it in his hand, then he toed off his shoes, spread his stance and allowed her to shuck off his cargo shorts and underwear in one fell swoop. He stepped from his clothing. Came for her.

Kiara rocked back on her heels. Goodness, but he was magnificent. Much better than she'd expected. Her heart thumped.

Wyatt made a bed of their clothing and pulled her down on top of the pile, all while his mouth was stealing rough, hungry kisses.

They lay down side by side. He caressed her cheek and peered deeply into her eyes as if he saw the answer to the mystery of the ages. Kiara felt herself whisked into a vortex of pure energy. His tongue was light and cool, but it lit a burning fire down every nerve he touched.

In the dark mustiness of the cellar, surrounded by wine barrels and bottles, they were part of the history of this place, this island. Muted light from the wall sconces cast shadows over their faces. He straddled her body, one knee on either side of her hips, and gazed down at her.

His naked erection hardened and throbbed, and Kiara's nipples beaded tight in answering response. He was so big. So gorgeous.

Kiara reached up a trembling hand to touch her lips.

He looked down at her. She stared up at him, studying his face bathed in contrast. Shadows on one side of his face, light on the other. He lowered his lashes, giving a sultry, bad-boy appearance to his deep-chocolate-brown eyes.

"What's on your mind?" he asked.

"You," she said. "I'm wondering how you got into my life and turned it upside down so quickly. Three days ago I didn't even know you existed and now it feels as if I've known you forever."

"I feel the same way," he admitted.

"What's happened? How did it happen?"

"It doesn't matter," he said. "All that matters is that it did happen."

He rolled over to stretch out beside her, propping his head on one arm. He leaned in to kiss her, to caress his mouth over hers in the most perfect kiss anyone had ever given her. Sweet, warm and firm. Full of hope and promise.

A helpless moan rolled from her.

"Yes," he said. "That's exactly what I want to hear."

"Less talking, more kissing," she informed him.

"Yes, ma'am." He ran his tongue along the outside of her lips, outlining their shape.

She wasn't going to let him get away with teasing her.

He needed a dose of his own medicine. While he was fooling around with her mouth, she explored his most sensitive spots. When she lightly flicked his nipple with an index finger a soft shudder passed through him.

"Wicked." He breathed. "Who would have believed you were totally wicked?"

Kiara thrilled to his words because she had never, ever in her life been wicked. She was the good girl, the dutiful daughter and, until now, she'd thought she wanted it that way.

He kissed her again and she absorbed his heat. He tasted so good. She could seriously get addicted to his rich, masculine flavor. They played, tongues dueling, teeth nibbling. With each kiss, each touch, each indrawn breath, each tensed muscle, the tension climbed, burning higher, hotter, brighter, reaching fever pitch.

Her mind spun. She wanted him. Wanted him now. Wanted his hard body buried deep inside her until neither one of them knew where she ended or he began.

"I want you," she dared, reaching her hand down to touch his erect shaft. "Need you."

Wyatt pulled back. "No, no. You're moving too fast. Slow down."

Kiara whimpered her protest. "Tease."

"You love that about me." He chuckled.

"Humility is not your strong suit."

"You love that about me too."

In the distance, she heard the door to the wine cellar open, but her mind was so preoccupied she didn't really heed the noise.

"Kiara?" Maurice called, his voice anxious.

She froze in Wyatt's arms, when she should be

springing away from him. If Maurice caught them like this…

"Kiara! Are you down here?"

Kiara moved away from Wyatt, turned her back on him, blindsided, dumbfounded. Lost.

6

*Reserve: Term used to indicate
a wine of higher quality.*

MAURICE MET HER in the middle of the cellar, a deep
scowl on his face. "There you are." He looked harried.
"I've been calling and calling your cell phone."

Kiara ran a hand through her hair, tried to sober up
after the inebriation of the things she'd done with Wyatt.

"Your shoes are untied."

"Oh." Kiara bent to tie them, grateful for an excuse
to hide her face from her cousin. That's when she realized she didn't have her glasses. "What's up?"

"We have a situation."

"What kind of situation?"

"That cat I told you not to adopt—"

"What?" Alarm spread through her. She felt numb.
Please don't let anything have happened to the stray.
She knew she shouldn't have fallen for him, but she had.
"What's up with Felix?"

"Felix's caused a big problem."

Relief pushed out the alarm. "But he's okay?"

Grandfather shot a look at Kiara that said *Who is this guy?*

Kiara shrugged, sent him a silent message. *Let him do his thing.*

"Well," the woman said. "That filthy animal shouldn't be kept where wine is stored."

"The cat is a stray who showed up here, but you are one-hundred-percent correct. I do hope you'll forgive Bella Notte's oversight." Wyatt still had hold of her hand and he drew up a chair with his other hand to sit beside her wheelchair. Wyatt was giving the woman his full attention. He never looked right nor left. He didn't even blink. It was as if his entire world had narrowed to that woman.

He would make a brilliant politician.

"It's a dangerous situation," the woman said. "Not to mention bad luck to have a black cat cross your path."

"Black cats can be scary," Wyatt placated.

"My ankle could be broken, not merely sprained."

"It certainly could and you're probably very tired after a morning filled with wine-tasting. Am I right to assume that Bella Notte was not the first vineyard on your tour today?"

"It was my third stop," she admitted.

"I know when I go wine-tasting, my head gets a little fuzzy. I have a tendency to drink more wine than I taste." Wyatt chuckled. "But you look like a woman with a lot of willpower. I'm sure that you avoid getting tipsy at tastings."

"Absolutely," the woman said. The brightness in her eyes and the way the *ly* slid off her tongue told Kiara that yes indeed she *was* tipsy.

"That's really good, because being tipsy in those

killer Jimmy Choos might cause anyone to fall and hurt their ankle," he pointed out.

Jimmy Choos? How did Wyatt know what brand of shoes the woman had on? Kiara wouldn't know Jimmy Choo from a choo-choo train.

"They might be a bit too tall for wine-tasting," Janet conceded.

A bit? They were four-inch heels! Kiara stifled her outrage to keep from saying exactly that.

"We'll pay for your medical bills, of course, and we'd like to offer you a free return tour to the winery with a group of your friends. Maybe during harvest season so you can see the vineyards in full action."

Seriously? He was making offers on behalf of Bella Notte? Kiara was affronted, but at the same time admitted she would have made the same offer, and she had given him her permission to handle it.

"Are you single?" Janet asked, and then giggled girlishly. "I suppose that question was inappropriate."

"It wasn't inappropriate at all," Wyatt assured her. "And yes, I am single."

The woman swooned before Kiara's very eyes. "So am I."

"Isn't that a lovely coincidence," he said smoothly. "Perhaps we could get together sometime."

Seriously? He was asking her out? Jealousy nipped at Kiara. Not ten minutes ago he'd been about to have sex with her and now he was asking out this woman who might sue Bella Notte?"

"How about today?" Janet asked.

"Let's wait and see about your ankle."

Kiara gritted her teeth. She was just about to say something tacky when Janet said, "You know, it really isn't Bella Notte's fault that a stray cat jumped out of the shadows. I mean it could have happened anywhere."

"It could have," Wyatt agreed.

Kiara fumed. Actually, she was glad this had happened. Now she saw what a huge mistake she'd been about to make with Wyatt. Relief. That's what she felt. Relief that she'd escaped.

"If you just take care of my doctor's bill I don't think there will be a need for any litigation."

"From the moment I laid eyes on you I knew you weren't the kind of woman who would sue an honest, hardworking family like the Romanos over something they couldn't control."

"Of course not."

Kiara placed a hand over her mouth. Was the woman so oblivious to Wyatt's obvious machinations? He was catering to her worries to get her to drop her threat of a lawsuit. Couldn't she see through that?

Be glad she can't see through that.

"Janet, I'm going to stay right with you until the doctor comes to check you out, and then I'll escort you back to your lodgings. Are you staying here on Idyll?"

"I am at the Idyll Inn, room eleven."

"That's good."

There was a knock on the door and Maurice came in, followed by Dr. Foster. He was a thin man with a bushy beard and round wire-framed glasses. Kiara thought he looked a bit like Sigmund Freud. He was a holdover from the past, a doctor who still made house calls.

Everyone scattered to go about their business. Trudy went to take over with the rest of the tour group who'd been sent to mill around in the gift shop. Grandfather went to take Trudy's place manning the gift shop.

Grandmamma carried her lasagna offering back to the kitchen and Maurice left to back the van up to the door to give Janet a return lift to the inn.

The doctor examined his patient and, throughout it all, Wyatt held Janet's hand.

Kiara watched, arms crossed over her chest. Wyatt was amazing, but, of course, he excelled at getting women to do what he wanted them to do. Just as he'd had her shimmying out of her dress down in the wine cellar.

Kiara's face burned with shame. She couldn't believe she'd done that. Had no idea what had come over her.

What she couldn't figure out was why a guy like him wanted to be at Bella Notte and why he was so eager to help. Everyone in Kiara's family was open, honest and trusting. Not she. Maybe it was the skeptic in her, her scientific mind that led her to doubt everything until it was proven conclusively.

Maybe she was simply born distrustful. But her ability to see things objectively instead of romantically like every other Romano was what had brought the winery back from the brink of bankruptcy. It was the reason her family had put her in charge over Maurice, who was older, after her father got cancer. Maurice had been really angry about it, but the winery was truly a family affair and everyone but his own wife had voted for Kiara to helm Bella Notte.

She took her job seriously, but she had to admit her weaknesses. She didn't possess the necessary social skills to head off a potential lawsuit the way Wyatt had just done. She was a straight shooter. She got to the point and spoke her piece. Blunt, she'd been called.

The doctor finished his examination and diagnosed a

minor sprain. Somehow, Wyatt sweet-talked Janet into signing a waiver saying she wouldn't sue Bella Notte for her injuries. Then he wheeled her from the tasting room into the waiting van.

He paused at the doorway to whisper to Kiara, "I'm going into town to make sure Miss Hampton is comfortable, but when I return, carve a chunk of time from your schedule. You and I are going to have a long talk."

WYATT GOT JANET Hampton ensconced in her hotel and had a glass of wine with her. She told him her life story. How she'd been dumped by her rat-bastard boyfriend and had decided to go on a trip to clear her head. He let her cry on his shoulder, gave her a pep talk and left the inn feeling pretty proud of himself.

It wasn't until he was back at Bella Notte that he even remembered why he was here. He'd been so caught up in impressing Kiara that he'd forgotten he was supposed to be a spy. He put the glasses back on that he'd taken off while interviewing Janet. They felt artificial and heavy on his nose. He was starting to have second thoughts about this whole thing. Especially after what had happened between him and Kiara in the wine cellar.

"How did it go?" Grandfather Romano greeted him in the parking lot. Fierce green eyes, identical to Kiara's, fixed on him.

"Lawsuit successfully averted."

Grandfather Romano studied him so long Wyatt started to feel itchy. "You look like someone."

"Oh." Was the old guy on to him? Even though Wyatt himself wasn't in the wine business, his family was. And the wine community was a very small one. He'd been dumb to think he could fool the people at Bella

Notte for long. He wasn't a spy. He just liked having a good time and going undercover had sounded fun. Now it felt…well…*wrong.*

If the older man raised the alarm, and Kiara found out who he really was, Wyatt would never have a chance with her.

Never have a chance with her? What the hell did that mean? Chance for what? Hot sex? Beyond that, he never stood a chance anyway. As soon as she found out he was a DeSalme, everything was over.

Well, that bites.

Disappointment nibbled at him. Why?

"What's your name again?" Grandfather Romano asked.

"Wyatt Jordan."

"And you're a new intern?"

"I am."

"Bit old for an intern."

"Yes."

"Your age has served you well. You've got some sharp people skills."

"I appreciate the compliment."

The old man kept scrutinizing him. "You'll be good for her."

"Sir?"

"My granddaughter. She's a brilliant scientist and has a great head on her shoulders when it comes to business, but she works too hard. A charmer might just be what she needs. But if you hurt her, I'll hunt you down like a rabbit and dispatch you."

"Excuse me?" Wyatt swallowed.

The old man smiled jovially. "You heard me."

"I'm not—"

"Save the protests. I noticed the way you looked at her. More importantly, I saw the way she looked at you. Be careful, young Wyatt. You play fast and loose with her heart..." He paused to draw a finger dramatically across his throat.

"Got your message, Don Romano," he joked. "You won't have to put a horse head in my bed."

The old man burst out laughing. "You're a funny guy. I like you. Treat Kiara right and all will be well."

"I have no intention of hurting your granddaughter, sir."

"Good, good." He placed a heavy hand on Wyatt's shoulder. "Come to dinner."

He couldn't shake the feeling that Grandfather Romano knew who he was. "Pardon me?"

"Come to dinner tonight. Kiara's father and mother have returned from San Francisco. We're having a small celebration."

"Um...I'm not sure Kiara wants me there."

"Are you a man or a mouse?"

Wyatt drew himself up. He was a good four inches taller than the elderly man, but the senior Romano made him feel like a schoolboy. "A man. Definitely."

"My granddaughter is very willful. If you want to be with her, you must be stronger than she is."

"I can do that."

"Do you want another tip?"

"I'm all ears."

"Don't give in to her too easily. Romance is sweetest when you have to work for it."

IN THE LAB, Kiara squinted at the vine sample under her microscope. After Wyatt had left with their trouble-

some guest, she'd called the Idyll veterinarian clinic and
made an appointment to have Felix neutered, chipped
and vaccinated for the following morning. If she was
going to keep the naughty feline, it was time to assume
responsibility for his health care. Now, she was trying
hard to concentrate on her work. The past three days
had been very disruptive, from the arrival of the new
interns to the earthquake to Janet Hampton's accident
in the barrel room to her own inexplicable misbehav-
ior in the cellar.

She thought of Wyatt, how easily he'd turned a tricky
situation into a nonissue. How had this man come into
her life and so quickly inserted himself in it as if he belonged there? She'd only known him seventy-two hours.
What was with this sensual sensory overload that preoccupied her every time she looked at him? Thought
of him.

Kiara was unaccustomed to breathless physical re-
sponses that left her confused and irritated because they
were so unfamiliar and unwanted. But as she stared at
the vine sample and her mind wandered back to the
wine cellar, her nipples beaded beneath the thin cotton
material of her dress, her long hair trickled the backs of
her bare arms, she felt her pulse quicken as her body—
oh, who was she kidding, it was more than her body—
yearned with abject longing for something that could
rock her world as effectively as any earthquake.

For a whisper of a second—an infinite, empty
second—loneliness twisted her stomach. Immediately,
she shoved it aside. She understood, had no choice but
to understand, that her uncharacteristic impulses were
dangerous to her position as head of Bella Notte. She

was not free to let her emotions off the leash. Nor did she want that freedom.

All her life, she'd been surrounded by romantics and their fanciful myths and legends, and she'd never once been tempted to succumb to the allure of lore.

There was her great-grandparents' explosive romance that had sparked a town legend. Then her grandmother had been engaged to another man until her grandfather had come to school to pick up his nephew where her grandmother was the new schoolteacher. She broken up with her fiancé the very next day.

Her parents had met in San Francisco at a small Italian restaurant where her mother worked as a waitress. Kiara's father had been delivering wine and her mother showed him to the wine cellar at the same moment there had been a blackout. They ended up locked in the cellar for several hours. By the time they were rescued, they were engaged.

Maurice and Trudy met at a wine-tasting event. One look into each other's eyes and they went out for dinner afterward, and stayed up all night talking. Maurice sauntered into the vineyard the next morning and announced he'd found the woman he was going to wed. They married a month later and a year after that Mia was born.

Kiara was the odd woman out—as if she was a self-possessed island, her family the distant mainland with no bridge or boat to connect them—and she'd known it from early childhood. Although the family reveled in her uniqueness, they put her up on something of a pedestal, revered her level-headedness. It made it difficult to make a mistake without rippling repercussions.

It bothered her too, whenever she did slip from her

lofty perch. Her mistakes ate at her, kept her awake at night. So she buckled down, kept her nose to the grindstone and kept romantic liaisons light, few and far between. Emotionally, her heart was untouched, and physically, no man had ever roused her to the trumpet-blaring ecstasy so enthusiastically touted by novels and love songs and sappy greeting cards. Proving what she suspected all along—romance was bunk. Or at least it was for her. Was she some sort of genetic anomaly? Maybe she simply didn't possess the capacity to feel deep emotion.

You were feeling pretty deeply this morning.

That wasn't emotion. That was lust. Animal magnetism. Nothing more.

What dismantled her was that this behavior was so out of character for her. Never in her life had she been drawn to someone the way she was drawn to Wyatt.

How did she stop this feeling?

A soft knock sounded at the inside door that led into the main house. Her stomach jumped. Was it Wyatt? Had he finally come back from his trip to Idyll?

"Come in."

The door opened and her grandmother appeared. "Your parents are at the ferry," she said. "Maurice has gone to fetch them."

"I'm so happy Dad's in remission."

"We're having a surprise party. I didn't tell you because you're so busy, but I was wondering if you could help me in the kitchen."

"Sure thing, Grandmamma. What do you need?"

"I'm making tiramisu. Could you soak the lady fingers?"

She followed her grandmother down the long corridor to the main kitchen. Kiara had her own small, one-room apartment, complete with a tiny kitchen, just off the lab, but she often took her evening meals with the family.

She washed her hands and then made the espresso for soaking the ladyfingers while Grandmamma started beating egg yolks over a double boiler. She'd been lucky to grow up in a big, loving, extended family. She knew that, but sometimes she wondered if maybe being nestled so securely in the bosom of her loved ones was one of the things that made her so reluctant to venture into the outside world. Her sister, Deirdre, called their family smothering, but Kiara didn't see it that way. To her, making her living at the home where she'd grown up was an honor and a privilege.

"Did you know your great-grandmother Maria made this recipe for Giovanni on the very night he proposed?"

"Yes, Grandmamma," Kiara said, suddenly feeling sentimental. "But I'd love to hear the story again."

Grandmamma cocked her head at Kiara, a surprised smile curling up the corners of her mouth. "Oh, you were never one for the romantic stories. When your mother tried to read Cinderella and Snow White to you, you'd pull out your grandfather's field guide to butterflies and flowers. We knew even then that you were different from most girls, *caro*."

"I'm sorry."

"Kiara, no," Grandmamma scolded. "Never apologize for being who you are."

"But I'm not like the rest of you. There's not a romantic bone in my body."

"And yet, here you are, asking about the story of

Giovanni and his beloved Maria." Grandmamma's eyes twinkled.

Kiara poured hot coffee into a shallow bowl, and added half a cup of Kahlua. Then she took ladyfingers from the cookie jar on the counter. One by one, she soaked the delicate cookies in the liquid, then lined them up in neat rows along the bottom of a baking pan.

"So how did Great-grandfather Giovanni know that Maria was the one he wanted to take up to Twin Hearts?"

"Maria stepped off the ferry on that fine day in June. She'd come from Italy to visit her relatives. Giovanni was in the village buying flour. He took one look at her and he wanted her with a burning need unlike anything he'd ever felt before."

"Just like that?"

"Just like that. Maria was struggling with her bags, and Giovanni, with the flour flung over his shoulder, dropped it in the middle of the road and ran to help her."

"Sounds like a traffic hazard."

Grandmamma chuckled. "I suppose it well might have been. He touched her hand and Maria looked into his eyes and the rest is history."

"What about you and Grandfather? Was it love at first sight for you?"

Her smile grew sly. "Did I ever tell you he was naked the first time I saw him?"

Kiara's jaw dropped. "Grandmamma!"

Grandmamma held up her hands to her mouth and giggled. "He was skinny-dipping in the dawn. Like Maria, I was a newcomer to Idyll. I'd been hired to teach school in the village, and on the first morning I awoke in town, I opened my bedroom window and

looked out across the inlet and there he was. Whew."
She fanned herself. "My Nico was something to look
at in those days."

"I don't think I want to hear anymore," Kiara said.
"I can't imagine Grandfather skinny-dipping."

"It was planting season and he'd been working in the
vineyards all night and he'd gone to the ocean to cool
off."

"So what did you do?"

"I watched." Grandmamma laughed again. "I was
late for my first day of school."

"So what happened when you met face to face?"

"He came to school to pick up his nephew from my
class that very afternoon. He stood in the door and when
our eyes met it was an instant bond so deep and solid
that nothing could break it."

"You know that really sounds far-fetched," Kiara
said, even as she thought, *That's exactly how I felt the
minute I looked at Wyatt.* Could it be this thing between
them was something more than the hot rush of lust?
More than mere chemistry?

*It's illogical and unscientific. You don't believe in
that romantic nonsense, remember?*

No, but part of her wanted to. Was that so wrong?
Not wrong, just not real. As long as she understood it
was a fantasy and not reality, then might it be okay to
indulge in a little wish fulfillment?

"We've been married fifty-three years. What more
proof do you need than that? You know the same is true
for your mother and father. Follow your heart, *caro*. It
will never lead you astray."

7

*Vineyard wisdom: The deeper the roots,
the sturdier the vines.*

DINNER WITH THE Romanos was a lively affair. It was a
true celebration in every sense of the word, with Kiara's
father, Gino, present and his cancer in remission. Kiara's mother, Beth, stayed by his side the entire night,
holding her husband's hand and reaching over from
time to time to pat his cheek as if unable to believe their
extreme good fortune.

Wyatt dressed for dinner, putting on the only decent
clothes he'd brought with him on his undercover assign-
ment—a pair of simple khaki slacks and a button-down
white shirt. He left the top two buttons undone and wore
a plain brown belt with brown deck shoes. Hoping he
didn't look too put together for a winery intern, he'd
gone to the house feeling more nervous than he'd felt
since that first morning in the tasting room.

Kiara seemed genuinely surprised when her grandfather led Wyatt into the kitchen, but she hadn't com-
mented on him being invited to dinner, had simply

greeted him with a subdued hello and gone back to putting platters of food on the table. Had she forgotten he told her that they needed to have a long talk?

One glimpse of Kiara and he felt a hot rush of desire so intense he had to school his features into a mild expression for fear the astute people in the room would see exactly what he was feeling.

She wore slim black jeans—a sexy change from the shapeless dresses—and a long blue V-neck tunic that molded softly against her breasts and showed off her amazing cleavage. Her hair was down for once, tumbling around her shoulders in a fiery cascade instead of pulled back into a ponytail. She'd even put on a bit of makeup—lipstick, mascara and blush—and had exchanged the gold studs for dangly crystal earrings. When the light caught the crystals, it sent a halo of tiny rainbows dancing around her ears. She looked like some mythical fairy princess.

He thought about that morning in the wine cellar. Had it been only such a short time ago? It felt like aeons since he'd touched her bare skin, kissed those sweet lips.

The big oak table was laden with delicious home-made Italian fare—stuffed mushrooms, lasagna Bolognese, eggplant rollups, pasta with sausage and tomatoes—all served family-style. They started the meal with antipasto of Genoa salami, kalamata olives, roasted garlic, pepperoncini, artichoke hearts, mozzarella and provolone sprinkled with olive oil. There was tiramisu and gelato for dessert and wine flowed freely. Having spent most of his adult years in Europe, Wyatt felt right at home.

Kiara was in rare form. She laughed and made jokes and hugged her father every time she hopped up from the table to retrieve more wine or tea. She ruffled the hair of her young cousins, teased Maurice about the Janet Hampton incident, girl-talked to her cousin-in-law Trudy, her mother and her grandmother. He'd never seen her so relaxed and wished he could help her feel like this all the time. He was just beginning to fathom the scope of the stress she'd been under, between her father's illness, the winery's financial trouble and taking over the helm at Bella Notte.

The food was superior, the company more so. Wyatt looked around the table. Grandfather Romano sat at the head of the table, his wife at the foot. Maurice sat to Grandmother Romano's right and beside him was Trudy. Juliet sat beside her mother. Directly across the table from Maurice sat his other three children. Mia was to the left of her grandmother, Elliott in between her and Samuel. Kiara's mom sat next to Samuel. Kiara's dad was next to her mom. Wyatt was seated across from Kiara's dad and to the right of Grandfather Romano. Kiara sat between Wyatt and Juliet. They all made him feel as welcome as if he were a long-lost relative.

And that made him feel guilty.

They lingered over the meal until Kiara's father suggested an evening walk through the vineyard. Everyone pitched in to clean up the leavings of the meal, then the entire bunch headed for the vineyard.

He hesitated, not knowing if he was wearing out his welcome or not.

"Come along, Wyatt." Grandfather Romano motioned for him to follow.

His own family was a bit fractured. His parents had divorced when he was a kid, not long after DeSalme Vineyards went corporate, and they'd both remarried.

His mother lived in Alaska with Lars the crab fisherman, and his father, along with wife number three, lived on the French Rivera. Wyatt saw him more often, but he tried to keep his distance from his young stepmother who had a tendency to grab him inappropriately when his father wasn't looking. He loved his brothers and their families, but he didn't have much in common with them. Scott and Eric lived and breathed the corporate lifestyle. They loved making money hand over fist. Not that there was anything wrong with that. Wyatt just had different priorities. Or at least he used to. Those had begun to shift when his brothers had called and asked him to do this thing for them, made noises about him coming to work for the company. That was a first. At last, his family needed him for something. Wyatt just had different priorities. Sailing his yacht, working as a PR consultant whenever he wanted to. Enjoying his friends and the beauty of the Greek Isles. Or at least he used to.

But after only three days here at Bella Notte, this was more like what he really wanted—close-knit, comfortable, dedicated to producing excellent wines, not just making money for money's sake.

Since when did you want that?

Since he'd first looked in Kiara's eyes.

It disturbed him, these thoughts. He felt as if he'd shucked his skin and slipped into someone else's, and it was a disconcerting notion.

The vineyards were so quiet, peaceful. He noticed everyone but the children were holding hands— Grandfather and Grandmamma Romano, Gino and Beth, Maurice and Trudy. That left him and Kiara not touching. Maurice and Trudy's four kids darted through the grapevines, playing tag as the sun simmered on the horizon. The days were at their longest. Everyone's shadows hung from their heels, tall and skinny.

The old, nearly forgotten memory was upon him again. The green-eyed, auburn-haired girl he'd plowed into at his grandfather's vineyard so many years ago. Did he have a mental template from the past that made him think Kiara was something special? Was this all some crazy fractured childhood illusion of the perfect girl?

Wyatt glanced up and found Kiara's eyes on him. Ah, this was no girl. She was one-hundred-percent woman, all rounded curves and knowing eyes. He wanted her in his bed—*oops, you're sharing bunk beds with Steve*—okay, in her bed, in the vineyards, in the wine cellar. Any-damn-where he could get her.

He gave a brief, honest smile and she rewarded him with a glowing grin, bright as those rainbow-inducing earrings. He thought about what her grandfather had told him.

Don't give in to her too easily. Romance is sweetest when you have to work for it.

Up ahead of them in the row of grapes, Beth rested her head on Gino's shoulder and they stood swaying together as one, watching the setting sun. Gino's arm went around his wife. Wyatt felt embarrassed to witness this relentlessly tender moment between a husband and wife who'd just come through the staggering challenge of a serious illness.

Then for no reason at all, a lump rose in his throat. What was that all about? He wasn't a sentimental guy. Why the sudden mush of melancholia? This wasn't his family.

That was the thing, wasn't it? His father and his mother didn't have this kind of deep-rooted relationship. They'd quit on their marriage. Quit on each other. And they hadn't gone through anything a quarter as challenging as what the Romanos had been through. What gave some couples stick-to-it-ness? Was it genetics? DNA? Was his parents messy love life any indication that he too, was seriously flawed when it came to love? Was that why he'd never been able to feel anything more than surface emotions for the women he'd dated? Or—please God, if You're up there—could true intimacy be found and nurtured by anyone, no matter what their heritage?

From the time he was a young kid, he'd learned that keeping things light and lively made the people around him happy. He'd been the class clown, then, later, the daring swashbuckler. Showing off, grabbing attention any way he could. Racing cars too fast. Bungee-jumping. Snowboarding. Skydiving. He had the money and means to pursue whatever interest caught his fancy. Always looking for fun, fun, fun. Never stopping long enough to let pain catch up with him.

For the first time, it dawned on him how empty his life was with his racecars and his yacht and the Rolex and string of girlfriends. He'd been trying to fill his life up with things and activities and a revolving door of people just to keep from feeling too deeply.

What was his life going to be like when he was Gino's age? Would he be like his own father, sugar daddy to a woman young enough to be his daughter? A woman destined eventually to take him for as much money as she could and then clear out when a younger,

handsomer face came along? Everyone but his dad
could see the writing on the wall.

Wyatt took a deep, sobering lungful of air. Inhaled
the scent of good, honest earth and knew he didn't deserve to breath it. He'd been glib and wasteful and self-
indulgent, and he suddenly wanted to change that more
than anything. He wanted to belong here.

It was an unexpected realization and he knew it was
all due to the woman standing beside him.

Kiara lowered her eyelids, but she was still watching
him. What was she thinking? Was her mind on grape
yields and micro-oxygenations, or was she, like him,
thinking of something far more philosophical?

Probably not. She wasn't the philosophical type. Her
mind ran to more solid corners—concrete, provable
corners with definite outcomes.

Then he saw her lick her lips and thought, *ah-ha*.
She was thinking about sex.

The events of that morning came rushing at him.
How he'd held her naked in his arms. How they'd been
within minutes of making love before Maurice had
interrupted them. What would have happened if they
had made love? Would they now be holding hands?

The rest of her family kept walking, but Wyatt and
Kiara stayed behind by unspoken consent, saying nothing, just looking at each other. Twilight edged around
them, casting her in cool shadows. The dying sunlight
swirling through her auburn hair made it glint fiery-
red and tinted her milky skin.

It was as if he'd been killing time with those other
women, just waiting for Kiara to show up. As if somehow his subconscious mind had *known* she was out

there and had prevented him from ever feeling like this with anyone else.

Whimsical, that thought, but he couldn't shake it. More to the point, he didn't want to shake it. Every instinct in his body pushed him to carry her off somewhere private and finish what they'd started. It would be so simple. So natural.

He wanted to claim her, make her his. Which was startling. He'd never been possessive toward a woman. The emotion turned him every which way but loose.

Don't give in to her too easily. Romance is sweetest when you have to work for it.

He strolled over, put his hand on her shoulder and peered deeply into her eyes. "Kiara," he said.

"Yes?" she whispered.

"I have something to ask of you."

"What's that?"

"Let me out of the lab. I want to work in the vineyards."

She was visibly startled. "You don't want to work with me?"

"Oh, I want to." He reached out to trace a finger over her lips. "That's the problem. I want to too much."

She took a step back, clearly rattled. "I don't understand."

"The thing that happened this morning in the cellar—"

"Was a mistake," she finished quickly.

He forced a sigh of relief. He prayed her grandfather was right. That playing hard to get was the way to land Kiara. If not, this whole thing could blow up in his face. "Do you really think that?"

"Of course it was a mistake. We were acting on impulse and that's never a good thing. Thank heavens Maurice showed up when he did."

"Yes," he said, but didn't mean it.

"And you're right," she went on. "The vineyard is a much better place for you. I'll pick another intern as an assistant. Perhaps that enthusiastic young blonde. What's her name?"

"Lauren."

"Yes. I think that would be a much better fit."

"You're absolutely right."

"Great."

"Fantastic."

"Terrific."

What was he doing? By putting himself in the vineyard, he was not only placing distance between himself and Kiara, but he was losing out on some prime spying.

Except Wyatt knew that in his heart, he'd already given up on that. Let his brothers deride him. There was something much more important at stake than a tiny portion of DeSalme's market share. The company would survive losing Sonoma's Best of the Best Award.

But Bella Notte? They might not.

KIARA HAD NO idea what was going on with Wyatt. He ran hot as lava one minute, cool as the ocean breeze the next.

Fickle. The man was fickle and she certainly didn't need that. But what if he was just as confused as she was by this undeniable attraction? Maybe he'd figured out what an unlikely couple they were—the scientist and the slacker—and he was getting out while the getting was still good.

She couldn't blame him. She should be grateful

really. It was the smart thing to do. Sever the connection before either one of them got electrocuted. Disaster successfully averted.

Except for the fact she couldn't sleep.

Insomnia was no stranger. With a mind chock-full of the details of precision viticulture—micro-oxygenation, reverse osmosis, spinning cones, evaporators—Kiara often had trouble sleeping. Her science littered her mind with chemistry and biology and botany like a playroom floor cluttered with Lego and Barbies and little green plastic army men, arms raised in constant battle. Her work was her play.

Except all that had changed since Wyatt's arrival.

Oh, her insomnia was still there, but the cause, that had changed.

Equations and formulas and experiments no longer danced in her head, keeping her awake. Now Wyatt prowled her nights. Images of him flashed through her head almost constantly and there was little defense against them—the way his dark hair fell rakishly over his forehead, the sound of his rich laughter bubbling up from his chest like a free-flowing spring, the feel of his five-o'clock shadow against the tips of her fingers, the extravagant taste of his lips.

He was always in her mind and she couldn't escape. Not even in sleep. For when she slept, she dreamed. And her dreams were even more vivid than her daytime fantasies.

In the lab, her new intern Lauren turned out to be a bubbly asset, eager to do whatever needed done, oftentimes anticipating Kiara's needs and doing it before she could even tell her.

Two weeks went by. Kiara stayed longer hours in

the lab. Burning the candle at both ends, working on new, organic methods of keeping the grapes healthy, dreaming up marketing campaigns for wider distribution after Decadent Midnight won the Best of the Best Award. She arose before dawn, got into bed long after midnight. Sometimes she didn't go to bed at all, just took catnaps at her desk.

Felix came through his neutering with flying colors and he became the exemplary pet, often lying curled at her feet, taking catnaps with her. He was the perfect male companion. She tried to convince herself that he was the *only* male companion she needed, but her body wasn't buying it.

Her body craved Wyatt.

Because of that, she did her best to stay out of the vineyards, sending Lauren whenever she could, and when business forced Kiara there, she would tell herself she was not going to look around for Wyatt. But then, damn, if she didn't lift her head and search among the interns tending the vines until she spied his form toiling in the hot sun.

Then her stupid pulse would kick up a notch and she'd duck her head and rush back to the lab, forgetting why she'd come to the vineyard in the first place.

It was an uncomfortable way to live and she did it for two weeks. Pushing, pushing, pushing, working, working, working herself to exhaustion, anything to keep from dwelling on Wyatt.

On the twenty-first of June, she woke with a summer cold. Headachey, miserable congestion, sneezing. She tried to push herself from the bed, but dizziness assailed when her feet hit the floor, sending her falling back among the covers. She called Lauren, and told her to spend the day in the vineyard with Maurice instead of coming to the lab, and then, feeling resentful of the illness in particular and Wyatt in general, went back to sleep.

She woke sometime later to the sound of a gentle knocking on her door. Groggily, she sat up. It was probably her mother or Grandmamma. Lauren must have spread the word that she was ailing. Kiara sighed. She hated to be fussed over.

"Come in," she called and drooped against the pillow.

The door opened, but it was neither her mother nor her grandmother.

Wyatt stood there, backlit by sunshine so that she couldn't see his face, only his hard-muscled form. "I heard you were under the weather."

"Just a cold," she said, but with her stopped-up airways it came out sounding like, "Jussa cole."

"You've been working too hard."

She couldn't argue.

"And not sleeping," he said, coming into the room and closing the door behind him.

Now she could see his face and a familiar shivery thrill rushed over her. Probably just running a fever. "How do you know that?"

"I've seen the light on in the lab at all hours for the last week."

"What have you been doing up wandering the grounds at all hours for the last week?"

He shrugged. "Stretching my legs."

So he hadn't been sleeping either. She canted her head, studying him. He carried a brown paper bag.

"I brought you something." He pulled out a long flat

box wrapped up in white foil paper and tied with a red velvet ribbon.

"You got me a gift." Touched, Kiara placed a hand over her heart.

"Just a little something." He perched on the bed beside her and handed it to her. "A get-well present. Go ahead. Open it."

Here he went with the mixed messages again. You didn't give a gift to someone you were avoiding having a relationship with.

Don't read anything more into this than what's there. It's a mere token.

"Kiara," he chided softly. "What's wrong?"

"Nothing. Absolutely nothing's wrong." She drooped, struggled to deal with the feelings churning inside her.

He hooked an index finger under her chin and raised her face up to look at him. "You can talk to me. Does gift-giving make you uncomfortable?"

"No. Yes. I don't know what you expect of me."

"You're overthinking again. Don't you ever rest that poor tired noggin?" He leaned closer and dropped a kiss on her forehead.

The touch of his lips heated her up inside.

"I didn't get you a gift."

"Why would you? Just open it up. Then you can make up your mind whether the gift is inappropriate or not."

Her fingers skimmed over the bow. Her heart stumbled, unsteady.

"Listen, clearly I've made you uncomfortable. That was not my intention. I saw this in a store window in the village and immediately thought of you. It was an impulse buy. No big thing."

Kiara opened the box. Inside, nestled in tissue paper,

lay a wristwatch. Nice white leather band, but not too expensive. She let out a pent-up breath. It was an attractive, but fairly ordinary watch, until she looked at the face.

Every number on the white-faced dial was a bold red five. Her eyes met Wyatt's.

A playful grin tilted his lips. "It's a reminder that somewhere in the world it's after five o'clock. Whenever you look at the watch I want you to remember the workday should end at five. After five, it's time to relax, take care of yourself and enjoy the fruits of your labor."

It was a perfect gift. Her throat clotted with emotion.

"Do you like it?" He sounded anxious.

"I love it."

"No more burning the midnight oil. No more making yourself sick."

"All right."

"I mean it."

"I'll try," she amended.

"Promise?"

"I promise."

"Good," he said. "I brought you some else."

"What is it?" She leaned over and tried to get a look inside the paper bag.

"Chicken noodle soup."

"You didn't have to go to all that trouble."

"I didn't. Your grandmother did." He pulled the container of soup from the bag. "C'mon. Let me fluff your covers so you can sit up straight to eat this."

Kiara set up, while Wyatt arranged her pillows. She sank back against them. "I had other opportunites you know."

"What? You had other guys bringing you soup and watches?" he teased.

"I mean professionally."

"I never said you didn't."

"No, but I see it on your face. You're wondering why I'm here at this struggling vineyard when I could be working for a big corporation where I could have sick leave and a pension."

"It might have crossed my mind," he admitted.

"I've had all kinds of opportunites."

"Oh?"

Why was she telling him this? It had to be the fever. *Shut up, Kiara.* "I got a fellowship to study in one of the premium wineries in France."

"Uh-huh."

"When I matriculated college, one winery even offered me a six-figure salary to come work for them in Napa. I could have had a pension, paid health insurance, vacation and sick time."

"Why did you turn them down?"

Emotion bubbled up in her. Tears misted her eyes. "Because I love my family and Bella Notte with all my heart and soul. This place is in my blood and bones. It's where I belong. This is what I was put on earth to do. I've always known it."

"No doubts, ever?"

"None."

"Wow."

"Wow what?"

"I've never loved anything with that kind of passion. Never felt that kind of loyalty toward anyone."

"That's sad," she whispered.

"I know," he said. A sorrowful expression flickered across his face and it tugged on her heartstrings. Quickly, he turned away, opened the soup container, took a spoon from the bag and ladled up a mouthful. When he turned back around, his charming smile was firmly affixed.

"Open up."

"You're not going to feed me."

"I am."

"This is silly."

"If you won't take care of yourself, someone has to do it."

"Wyatt, I can feed myself."

"Ah, but wouldn't it be a lot more romantic if you let me feed you?" he cajoled.

"There's nothing remotely romantic about this. I'm sick with a summer cold, my nose is red, my hair is a mess and—"

"You look gorgeous."

"You are such a liar."

"Now you're denigrating my taste in convalescing invalids?"

She had to smile. The man was completely irresistible.

"Open up." He held out the soup-spoon loaded with chicken, carrots, celery, onion and egg noodles.

Feeling dorky, she reluctantly opened her mouth.

He gently slipped the spoon past her teeth, as if he'd spent a lifetime spoon-feeding her.

Their gazes locked. He was sitting on the edge of the bed, turned toward her, his butt against her thigh. Yes, sure the covers were between them and so was the material of his shorts, but it felt so intimate, so cozy.

Dammit.

He was right. It *was* romantic, the fact that he was willing to brave the chance of catching her cold. The truth that he was looking at her as if he did indeed think she was gorgeous, mussed hair, running nose and all. The notion that he was the kind of guy you could trust to take care of you when you were sick, well, it was dangerous stuff.

Especially when she thought he would be the kind of guy to turn tail and run at the sight of anything unpleasant. But that wasn't the case. He was here and he didn't seem the least bit repulsed by seeing her at her worst.

"What are you thinking about so fiercely?" Wyatt asked.

"I'm wondering how I can increase the yield from the current crop of muscat grapes," she lied, not wanting to tell him that she was thinking about how grateful she was that he was here.

"No, no," he scolded. "No thinking about work."

"That's like telling me not to breathe,'" Kiara said.

"You can control what you think about."

"You make it sound so easy."

"It is easy."

"Ha!"

"You push yourself too hard," he said. "No wonder you're sick. When was the last time you took the day off?"

Kiara frowned. "I do better if I don't take off."

"You're not a superwoman. Everyone needs a break."

She waved in the direction of the lab. "I have too much to do—"

"If you burn out, you'll be no good to anyone. I want you to promise me something else."

"What's that?"

"As soon as you're feeling better you'll take a day off to recharge your batteries."

"That's not going to happen. If I miss several days because of this cold I can't afford to take another one off."

"If you don't take a day off, you're not going to heal properly. When was the last time you did something just for yourself?"

"It's been a while."

"You give your interns two days a week off, why don't you feel entitled to do the same for yourself?"

"There's too much to be done."

"One day," he said. "I'm talking twenty-four little hours that are all about you."

The thought of taking a day off, of letting her mind run free, of relaxing and enjoying herself was so tempting. Too tempting. She hadn't done that since her father had been diagnosed with stage-three lymphoma and he'd stepped down as head of Bella Notte and she'd assumed his role as head of the business.

She'd known what she was getting into. But doing her job of creating the best wine, and his job of providing for an extended family of this size was a lot for anyone. Especially when she was only thirty. She should be out dating, mating, maybe even building a family of her own.

There's plenty of time for that, argued her sensible side.

But the side of her that she kept tamped down tight, whimpered. *Don't I ever get to have any fun?* It was that part of her that did not resist when Wyatt said, "Next Saturday you're coming with me."

"Oh, I am, am I?"

"Yes."

"What if I say no?"

"I'll get your whole family on my side."

She had no doubt that he'd do it too. "Where are we going?" she asked, charmed in spite of herself. "What are we going to do?"

"You leave the fun up to me. That's my strong suit."

To her surprise, Kiàra nodded. "Okay, I'll do it, but only under one condition."

"What's that?"

"You give me that spoon and let me feed myself."

8

Balance: When no part of a wine's flavor stands out too much.

KIARA CHEATED. SHE didn't stay in bed for the duration of her cold, on the third day she was feeling much better and spent a few hours in the lab, and to compensate, loaded up on vitamins. Later in the day, she lay propped up in her bed to pay the bills. It was a bit concerning to see that she was barely staying in the black, but still, they weren't in the red.

"All that's going to change," she told Felix, who was stretched out across her legs playing with a piece of balled-up paper she'd tossed aside while working on the figures. "When we win the Best of the Best. Are you prepared for success?"

Felix meowed and burrowed underneath the covers.

"I take that as a yes."

She wasn't even going to let herself consider what would happen if they didn't win the award. She was so secure in the excellence of Decadent Midnight, she'd put all her eggs in a single basket. If for some bizarre reason they didn't win, well, she'd be seriously scrambling to make ends meet. She'd only made it this far buoyed by the promise of the exceptional wine. It sold well here at Bella Notte and they had a respectable mail-order business, but they had to reach a wider market soon or the long-term viability of the family winery was in serious jeopardy.

By Friday, she was almost one-hundred-percent her old self and she had to admit she was excited about taking a day off, and was wondering what Wyatt had planned.

Just before dawn on Saturday morning, a knock sounded on her bedroom door. "Kiara?" her mother called from the other side of the door.

Kiara yawned, stretched. "I'm awake."

"Wyatt is here to pick you up for your date."

Date! What had he told her mother? They weren't going on a date. It was merely an outing that they were going on together, but she hadn't expected him to show up this early.

Kiara sprang from the bed, ran a hand through her messy hair and then flung open the bedroom door. "Mom, it's not a date. I just need a day off and he's taking me..." It sure sounded like a date when she put it like that.

"Okay, dear," her mother soothed, stepping into her room. "It's not a date."

Why had she agreed to this? What had she been thinking? She'd been indulging her lazy side. That's what she'd been doing. She squared her shoulders and opened her mouth to tell her mother to tell Wyatt that she was calling off the excursion. "Sorry," she mumbled. "I didn't mean to bite your head off."

Her mother smiled. "I'm just so happy you're taking the day off, Kiara. I've been so worried about you."

"Mom, you don't need to worry about me."

"You've been sick."

Kiara waved hand. "With a summer cold. Nothing to be alarmed about."

"You must start taking care of yourself. I fear your father's struggle to keep Bella Notte going is the very thing that contributed to his cancer. He never took a day off either. Never rested. Now he's been forced to reevaluate the life he was living. I didn't begrudge him his ambitions, but he never stopped to smell the roses. We live in one of the most beautiful places on earth and it wasn't until he had to face his own mortality that he's come to realize there's a benefit to slowing down. I don't want you to wait until you're in your fifties and your health is damaged before you understand that you have to take care of yourself before you can take care of anyone else."

"Yes, Mom."

Her mother studied her for a moment. "Wyatt is good for you. Do you know that you smile a lot more often since he's come to stay with us?"

"Do I?"

Her mother reached out to tuck a strand of hair behind Kiara's ear. "I like him."

I like him too.

"He just might be a keeper."

"Mom."

"Okay, okay, I know it's none of my business, but you know you have a tendency to run guys off."

"I don't run guys off."

"When you're dating a guy, you don't pay him much attention."

"I'm not a lapdog, Mother."

"Men like it when you pay them attention."

"I don't want a man that needs to be petted and preened."

"I didn't mean it like that. I'm messing this up. Wyatt's a nice guy. I like him. You could do a whole lot worse. That's all I'm saying."

"Duly noted."

"Grandmamma likes him too. She's making him French toast."

Kiara groaned. "You're feeding him breakfast?"

"Well, honey, you are leaving him waiting."

"Because he didn't tell me he was going to be here at the butt crack of dawn."

"Kiara, language."

"Sorry. I'll be there in just a minute. Try not to tell him too much about my childhood and whatever you do, don't let Grandmamma get out the photo album."

"Um, we might already be too late on that one."

"Tell him he brought this on himself for not telling me when he was going to be here."

Beth chuckled and disappeared.

Kiara hurried through her morning routine, and then dressed in white denim shorts and a red scoop-neck T-shirt. She was going to wear sandals, and then realized it had been months since she'd bothered with a pedicure and instead jammed her feet into sneakers. Maybe she should start taking time out for a little more pampering. She put on a dab of mascara and lipstick. Once finished, she appraised herself in the mirror.

Her hair. She had to do something with her hair. It

stuck out at all angles. She didn't have time to wash and blow-dry it. Wyatt was downstairs alone with her family. No telling what tales they were regaling him with. Quickly, she pinned her hair up in a French twist. It looked nice. Jewelry. Maybe she should wear some jewelry.

Oh, God, it *was* a date.

This is not a date. When was the last time she'd been on a date?

Stop it. Calm down. If you can run a winery, you can go on a simple date. So what if it's a date? You're entitled. You're young and single and hardworking.

Yes, but Wyatt worked for her. He was her intern. The balance of power tipped toward her.

What's wrong with that? It's one day. It's not like you're going to sleep with him or anything.

She thought of that day in the cellar and a sudden thrill sent goose bumps spreading over her arms.

Are you?

What was so bad about a summer fling? Fraternizing with an intern might not be the smartest thing in the world, but, honestly, it wasn't like they had long-term potential as a couple. He was a good-looking gadabout, a fun-loving slacker. There was no future there. He was leaving at the end of the season. But fun? She had a feeling that Wyatt could provide that in spades.

She stepped to the bedside table, picked up the whimsical five-o'clock watch he'd given her, and strapped it on her wrist. Then she reached far into the back of the drawer, pulled out a condom and slipped it into the pocket of her shorts.

Just in case.

Taking a deep breath to bolster herself, she went

downstairs and found Wyatt at the breakfast table
eating French toast with maple syrup, drinking a cup
of espresso and chatting with Grandmamma Romano.
A family photo album lay open on the table between
them.

"And here's Kiara when she was seven helping her
father cut back the grapevines. Look at that face, so
determined and headstrong even then. She wasn't going
to let that grapevine get the best of her."

"She wore glasses at seven?"

"She had to get glasses when she was just three. Poor
little thing. She was so tiny and yet so fierce, those big
glasses perched on her baby face. It broke my heart to
see her strapped with a disadvantage at such a young
age."

"Near-sightedness is not a disadvantage, Grandmamma." Kiara rushed across the room, to Wyatt she
said, "I'm ready to go if you are."

"She's embarrassed," Grandmamma said. "Our
Kiara is full of pride."

"Wyatt doesn't want to hear about my childhood."

"Oh," Wyatt drawled, his long legs stretched out in
front of his chair. "That's where you're wrong. I love
imagining what you were like as a kid."

"The same as what she is now," her mother called
from the stove. "She was such a little mother to her
younger sister and cousins. She liked being in charge
from the very first. We've butted a few heads over the
years. Haven't we sweetheart?"

This was turning into a fiasco. She didn't want Wyatt
knowing all the gory details of her childhood.

"Wyatt." She pointed at her watch.

"Slow down," he said. "That's the point of this day. Take a breather."

"Then why didn't you let me sleep in?"

Her mother slid a plate of French toast in front of her, along with a cup of espresso.

"Eat," Wyatt said before her mother had a chance to say it. Then he turned back to Grandmamma. "Tell me more."

Grandmamma held up another photograph. "Here's where she took first prize in the fifth-grade science fair. She was interviewed in the local paper. You should have seen her. Chest puffed out, eyes shining with happiness. We were so proud of her."

Kiara didn't miss Wyatt's lazy gaze zeroing in on her chest. She frowned at him, wrinkled her nose and took a long gulp of coffee. She needed an IV infusion of caffeine to get through this day.

She ate her breakfast as fast as she could while Grandmamma kept turning the pictures.

"Here's her prom."

"She went to the prom?" He sounded surprised. Granted, she wasn't the prom-going type, but did he have to sound so surprised?

"Oh, my, yes. Didn't she look so pretty in that purple dress?"

"Who's her date?" Wyatt asked, leaning over Grandmamma's shoulder for a closer look at the photograph. "Was that her first boyfriend?"

"No." Grandmamma sighed. "In high school, like now, Kiara didn't date much."

Kiara rolled her eyes to the heavens.

"That's her cousin Jerome," Grandmamma went on. "They were the same age."

"Jerome didn't go into the family business?" Wyatt asked.

"Jerome was killed," Kiara rushed to explain so Grandmamma wouldn't have to talk about her cousin. "In a scuba-diving accident."

"I'm sorry," Wyatt murmured.

Grandmamma's smile brightened as it always did when she was trying to ward off sad memories. "It was ten years ago…." she said as if time had healed all wounds. But the she added, "It still hurts."

"Sorry to hear that. Well, I'm ready to go if you are," Wyatt said to Kiara, clearly out of his league on the topic of tragic death. Hey, he'd started this. She ought to let him suffer. But she was suffering too.

"Done." Kiara finished her last bite of French toast, went to rinse her plate and put it in the dishwasher. She turned back to Wyatt and for the first time spied a picnic basket on the floor behind his chair.

"We're going on a picnic?"

"Among other things."

"What other things?"

"You don't have to know all the secrets of the universe," Grandmamma said. "This young man has prepared a nice day for you. Go, enjoy."

Kiara glanced at Wyatt skeptically.

"The day is all planned," he said. "Your only job is to relax and enjoy it. Can you handle that?"

"I don't know," she admitted.

When was the last time she'd let down her hair and stopped thinking about work for ten seconds? It had been so long, she couldn't remember. Long before her father got sick. Probably back in college, although she'd been pretty studious then too.

"C'mon." Wyatt put his hand to the small of her back and guided her outside into the dewy morning.

The sun was bumping over the horizon, casting the vineyards on the gently sloping hill behind the house in a soft Dreamsicle glow.

"Look at that." Beside her, Wyatt breathed deeply.

"At what?"

"Those beautiful grapes."

He was right. They were beautiful. She was usually so focused on the details that went into making a good wine that she rarely took the time to marvel over the vineyards the way tourists did. The way Wyatt was doing. As if this moment were somehow magical. He was right. She didn't appreciate the wonder of where she was privileged to live, of her unique heritage.

"Good," he said.

"Good what?"

"You're relaxing. I can see the tension draining from your face."

She raised a hand to her cheek. Was the stress that obvious on her? "Where are we going?"

"You'll see."

He took her elbow—and to Kiara's surprise, she let him—and he led her down the path to the Bella Notte Welcome Center. Parked outside the small stone building was a rack filled with bicycles built for two. They were rented out to tourists who wanted to tour the winding paths of Idyll Island. The bicycles had been Maurice's idea and to Kiara's chagrin they had been wildly popular. More romantic poppycock.

"Oh, no," she said. "Not the bicycles built for two. I don't do bicycles built for two."

"Why not?"

"Because it's corny."

Wyatt gave her that knee-melting, hundred-watt grin. "C'mon, corny can be fun."

"It's not my thing."

"So indulge me."

Kiara shook her head. She didn't know why she was resisting so hard. "Look, I don't know how to ride these things."

"Really? You've never ridden a two-seater?"

"That's what I mean by I don't do bicycles built for two."

Wyatt made a tisking noise. "You've been missing out."

"I suppose you've ridden one before."

"Hundreds of times."

"Hundreds?"

He shrugged. "Okay, maybe I exaggerate. Dozens."

"You're really weird, you know that?"

"Why? Because I know how to enjoy myself?"

"But a bicycle built for two?" She wrinkled her nose. "Really?"

"It's no different from riding a regular bicycle, you just have to get into a rhythm with your partner."

That's what worried her—getting into a comfortable rhythm with Wyatt, because the temptation was very strong, but she had no illusions about this man. He was a romantic, like her family. She knew better than to lay her heart on the line over chemistry. She was a clear-eyed scientist. She didn't let hormones and pheromones control her brain. She was in charge. Not biology.

Yeah? Keep telling yourself that. Maybe it'll stick.

Wyatt secured the picnic basket inside the wire basket attached to the front of the bike.

What would it hurt? A fling with him. Appease her biology and then scrub him right out of her mind. She knew this couldn't lead anywhere. She didn't want it to lead anywhere, but if he could help her to relax, could ease some of her tension, then why not just let it happen?

Why? Because it wasn't her way.

Maybe it's time to change your ways.

"Front or back?" Wyatt asked.

"What?"

"Do you want the front or the back?"

"Does it matter?"

"Well, in the front, you get to steer. You're in control. But the back is the power position. The motor, if you will."

Kiara stared at the bike. What would he do if she just turned and fled to the safety of the lab and reneged on her promise? "You've got stronger legs than I do, you take the back."

"I don't know about that," Wyatt said, his gaze roving over her legs. "You've got some awesome legs on you, lady."

Don't fall for his charms. Don't be like every other woman on the planet. Resist. Resist. "I like being in control. I'll take the front."

"Good choice." He took the bike from the rack.

They mounted the thing in unison and it took a wobbly minute to get accustomed to riding together, but they quickly got in sync and once they were underway, the bike sailed along with swift ease.

"Where to now?" she called to him over her shoulder, noticing how good it felt to have the wind ruffling through her hair on this early Saturday morning in June.

Don't fall for the romance of it. Of him. Don't you dare.

"Head for the marina."

"Are we going to the mainland?"

"I'm not giving away my secrets."

"You're a tease."

"Is that a problem?"

"How can I be in control if you don't tell me where we're going?"

"That's the surprise. You're not really in control."

Kiara tightened her fingers around the handlebars. "Turkey."

"Stop tensing up," Wyatt called to her.

"How do you know I'm tensing up?"

"I'm behind you. I can see the set of your shoulders."

"On the way home remind me to take the backseat."

"You? In the backseat? It'll never work."

"Why not?"

"Because if I'm in front I can't see your sexy butt. What do you think gives me the impetus to keep pedaling?"

"No fair, I wanna see *your* butt."

"You can see it on the boat."

"So we're going on the water. I have a clue!"

"Yes, Irene Adler, you have superior powers of deduction, especially considering that we're on our way to the marina."

"Who's Irene Adler?"

"Don't you ever read any fiction?"

"Hey, I went to college. I suffered through the requisite English classes."

"No Sherlock Holmes?"

"No."

"No fiction on your own?"

"I started *Grapes of Wrath*. I thought it was a book about vineyards. I couldn't get past the chapter-long treatise about a turtle crossing the road."

"The turtle was symbolic."

"I got that. It was still boring."

"I've got my work cut out for me," Wyatt said. "I'm considering having you kidnapped and deprogrammed."

"What for?"

"I think your brain has fermented with so much focus on winemaking."

"You're just jealous," she said.

"Of what?"

"My incredible powers of concentration."

His laugh ran out over the streets of the village, and Kiara acknowledged it had been a very long time since she'd had this much fun. Okay, so she'd been a bit quick to prejudge bicycles built for two.

They arrived at the marina and Wyatt directed her to park the bike beside a kiosk that rented sailboats.

"We're going sailing?" It had been years since she'd been sailing.

"We are."

"You know how to sail?"

"I do."

But, of course, he knew how to sail. He was that kind of guy, glib and smooth and charming. He was probably an expert sailor.

Her suspicions were confirmed the minute they were out on the water in the rented sailboat, the picnic basket stowed in the bottom of the hull between them.

The rays of the sun glittered off the water and the breeze was refreshing, but not cold. It was a perfect morning for sailing. The ocean rippled calmly, the sky was filled with innocent cloud puffs. The only sounds were the sail flapping in the wind and the steady clank of the rigging against the metal mast.

Along the shore came the sound of seagulls squabbling near the ferry landing. In no time they were away from Idyll and it occurred to Kiara that she was out here alone on the ocean with Wyatt. No other people. No distractions.

Just the two of them.

Delight shivered up her spine.

"Cold?" Wyatt asked.

"No."

"C'mere."

She eyed him suspiciously. "Why?"

"Come sit right here." He patted the transom of the boat beside him. "I'm going to help you relax."

"That sounds ominous."

"Why? Does relaxing scare you?"

"Frankly? Yes."

"Why?"

"You know you sound irritatingly like a three-year-old."

"That's because three-year-olds are very inquisitive. It's how they learn."

"So, following that line of reasoning, you are trying to learn what?"

"As much as I can about you."

"Why?"

"Ah." He grinned. "Now who's the three-year-old?"

"You got me."

He patted the spot again. "Come. Sit."

She edged over, keeping her body very rigid. "What are you up to?"

"You're going to love this, I promise."

"Love what?"

"Have you always been this suspicious?"

Had she? Probably.

"I won't bite, I promise." He paused. "Unless you want me to."

"Yeah, that's what the Big Bad Wolf said to Little Red Riding Hood."

"I thought you didn't believe in fairy tales."

"I don't."

"And here you are referencing one."

"It's not a happily-ever-after one."

"Red gets rescued. What's not happy about that?"

"From the wolf's point of view, he sort of got murdered. Not much happiness in that."

"So, you believe in dark fairy tales, but not the good ones."

"I'm a pessimist. Get used to it."

"You're missing out on so much."

"Like what?"

"Serotonin for one thing. The feel-good hormone."

"Technically, it's a monoamine neurotransmitter."

"Remind me not to argue with you about anything science-related."

"While you were reading Sherlock Holmes, I was reading biology textbooks for fun."

"You're strange."

"I read that pessimists actually have a better grip on reality than optimists."

"Hence the reason they are pessimists."

Kiara snorted. "I've spent my life surrounded by

optimists. Do you know how frustrating it is for twenty people to try and cheer you up when you simply want to worry, pout and sulk?"

"I'll let you worry, pout and sulk if you want to, just not today. Today is about having a good time. Relaxing. Letting go. If you clear your mind, your creativity will come back to you."

"I'm not creative, I'm a scientist. I deal in solid facts."

"Scientists are creative too. Where would the world be without Galileo and Sir Isaac Newton and Einstein? In fact, wasn't Einstein famous for some kind of quote about the imagination being more powerful than anything else?"

He had a point. She'd spent so much of her life resisting anything that smacked of whimsy that she'd closed herself off to many creative avenues. She'd tried so hard to stay levelheaded, her feet anchored to the ground. It was not an easy thing to do amidst the Romano clan.

"Shh," he said. "Close your eyes and let me take your worries away. Just for today."

Kiara did as he asked. Closed her eyes. Took a deep breath.

A second later she felt her skin tingle at Wyatt's touch. His fingers skimmed over the back of her neck, gently kneaded her tight muscles.

"When was the last time you had a massage?" he asked. "You've got knots upon knots."

"I've never had a massage."

"You're kidding?"

"Who has time."

"You do. Right now."

"Plus, I've never been all that keen on strangers touching me."

"Must wreak havoc with your love life."

"What love life?"

"Exactly," his said, his fingers firm but gentle as he rubbed the kinks from her neck.

In spite of herself, Kiara could feel her shoulders relaxing. Wyatt had a way of making a woman feel totally at ease around him. Which was disconcerting. For another thing, it had been so long since a man had touched her so tenderly that she soaked up the experience like a flower soaking up the sun. *You're so easy.*

He moved from her shoulders up her neck, his fingers finding sore spots and then dispatching them with steady, rhythmic strokes. Kiara moaned softly. This mini-massage felt so incredibly good. Sitting on the open water, the sailboat skimming over the rocking waves, the sun shining down on them, Wyatt's fingers working their magic, a sweet sense of perfection settled over her. She had been missing out. This felt sublime.

But if you did it all the time, it wouldn't be special. Just enjoy the moment, tomorrow you'll get back to work and everything will return to normal.

It was a valiant promise. She wanted to believe it. How great to be able to take a day off, recharge her batteries and go back to work. But she feared it was not going to happen that way. Feared that she wouldn't be satisfied with just one day. Feared that this was only going to make her want more, more, more. Wyatt was an easy person to grow accustomed to. Never mind that he was serious eye candy. He had a way of making her spirits lift simply by walking into a room.

His fingers were at her scalp, rotating circles through her hair. It felt so good, she moaned again and her spine curled against him as his fingers kneaded and stroked and caressed. It was the most intimate thing she'd ever done with a man besides sex.

"That's it," he murmured. "That's right. Let all your worries drain away. Just let go, Kiara. Let go."

And darn, if she didn't. At least for a few minutes. She thought of nothing but the pressure of his hands on her head and the warmth of the sun and the smell of the sea and the sound of the metal clip banging gently against the metal pole. It was sublime. One she'd remember for a very long time—long after Wyatt had vanished from her life.

Because he *would* vanish. He was an intern. They were total opposites in every way. And Kiara knew she was not the easiest person in the world to get along with. She'd always imagined she'd eventually marry. Someone like herself. Another scientist as absorbed with his work as she was with hers. A practical, measured man who would fall into lockstep with her.

But after meeting Wyatt, she wasn't sure she wanted that any longer. Her imagination conjured other possibilities for her future. Possibilities with a man who was *not* like her. A man who was so different he fascinated her at every turn. A man who was the yin to her yang. The other half who made her feel whole. The—

What in the hell was she thinking? That was romantic stuff. The Romano way. She'd fought against the impracticality of romantic myths her entire life.

Why do you think it's a myth, whispered a voice in the back of her head. *No one in your family has ever gotten divorced. Why do you fight it so hard against it?*

"You're tensing up again. Stop thinking about work. Look at your watch, it's after five."

She laughed. "It's hard not to," she said, reluctant to

tell him what she was really thinking. "My work isn't just a job. Wine isn't just in my blood and my bloodline. It's in my heart and soul as well. It's all I care about, besides my family."

"Now that sounds like something a die-hard romantic would say." Wyatt traced his index finger down the slope of her nose. "And along with what you told me that day I fed you soup confirms it. You are not one-hundred-percent clear-eyed scientist, Kiara. No matter how much you proclaim to the contrary. You are a complex and fascinating person, and I'm very happy you agreed to spend the day with me."

9

*Deep: Having lots of flavor that last a long
time and keeps changing in the mouth.*

THEY STOPPED FOR their picnic lunch on a small uninhab-
ited atoll. They could have been the only two people
in the world. Wyatt insisted Kiara let him take care of
everything. He wouldn't even let her spread out the
blanket in the field of wildflowers. It was odd. He
wasn't a caretaker by nature. Usually, the women were
the ones taking care of him and he had always enjoyed
being pampered.

But with Kiara, he wanted to take care of her. She
so badly needed someone to look out for her. Not that
her family didn't take care of her, but they depended
on her for their living. She needed someone who she
could depend on.

Wyatt wanted to be that guy.

The smile that curled on her face when she kicked
off her sneakers and sank down on the blanket made
him smile. She stretched, purred and propped herself up
on one elbow to watch him take their lunch items from

the picnic basket. The massage had done wonders for her. If she were his, he'd hire a masseuse to give her a rub-down once a week. She deserved the best.

"Thank you," she said.

"For what?" he asked, taking containers of rosemary chicken and potato salad from the basket.

"Insisting I get out of the lab. This is nice."

"My pleasure." Out came a jar of black olives, sun-dried tomatoes in olive oil and a loaf of crusty Italian bread.

When her gaze met his, he saw that her smile had changed. He'd never seen that particular look on her face, not even that morning in the wine cellar. It was part desire, part gratitude, part something else, and it made him want to know more about her. He wanted to dive deep into her smile and make a home there.

"You make me feel…" She paused.

"What?" He leaned closer.

"Like…" She tilted her head, considering. "That it's okay to be imperfect."

"Yeah, it's okay. We're all human. There's no such thing as perfect."

"I know that, but there's something that's always constantly driving me to strive for perfection."

"You put too much pressure on yourself."

"Maybe it's a birth-order thing," she said, reaching for a grilled chicken wing. "Being the oldest and all that."

"You have brothers and sisters?"

"One sister. Deidre's only twenty-two."

"Where's she?"

Kiara shrugged. "She's a bit of a drifter. But I'm also

the oldest girl out of a flock of cousins. In fact, Maurice is the only cousin older than I am."

"And yet he didn't turn out to have a problem with perfectionism."

"It was just a theory. How about you? Do you have any brothers or sisters?"

"Two older brothers."

"Ah, you're the baby of the bunch. That explains a lot."

"How's that?"

"Explains the smile for one thing."

"What's wrong with my smile?"

"You whip it out every chance you get. It's a bid for attention. The youngest child gets lost in the shuffle."

"So, you majored in psychology along with the science of winemaking?" he teased.

"Deidre's just like you. Charming, but irresponsible. There is something to birth order, Maurice aside."

Wyatt lowered his head. "Now, just because a person has some degree of charm does not make them irresponsible."

"Doesn't it?" She didn't back away.

"Perfectly said by a perfectionist."

"I'm judging again, aren't I?"

"That's not always a bad thing."

"I don't like being this way, it's a hard trait for me to break." She wiped her fingers on a napkin she plucked from the basket. "You help me in that regard. It's one of the things I like most about you."

"What else do you like about me?" He popped an olive into his mouth.

"Obviously, your deep humility."

He playfully tweaked her nose. "Okay, I'll go first and tell you what I like about you."

"Don't do that." She looked embarrassed, dipped her head and spooned a bit of potato salad in her mouth.

"I like how you blush when someone pays you a compliment. Like now."

She brought a hand to her cheek. "Stop looking at me."

"You make me feel like I've found a port in which to weather a storm."

"Oh." She laughed. "That sounds terribly sexy."

"You're making fun of me."

"I like your smile."

"You like that, huh?" Wyatt smiled.

"I like how you're showing me what it's like to be flexible and spontaneous."

"And I like how you set a good example. You keep me in line."

"This is starting to get mushy."

"I noticed that." Scary mushy. Mushy to the point where he was finding it a little hard to breathe. "Let's see what else we've got in this picnic." He pulled a bottle of Decadent Midnight from the basket.

"Isn't it early for that?"

"Look at your watch. It's after five."

"Well, isn't that handy?"

He reached for the corkscrew and the two wine flutes left in the basket. He poured it up, passed a glass to her, kept one for himself and recorked the bottle. "A toast."

She raised her glass.

"To the best damned dessert wine in the country."

"We have to wait until next month for that proclamation."

"I'm stating it now. Decadent Midnight is a winner."

"So are you," she said.

"You didn't think that about me the first day."

"We already know I have a problem with snap judgments."

"To second impressions," he said and they both took a second swallow of the sweet, impressive wine.

"Now," he said when they'd finished the wine and he'd put the glasses away. "I'm going to finish that massage I started in the boat. Give me your feet."

"No," she curled her feet up underneath her. "My nails aren't polished."

"Like I care about that." He wriggled his fingers in a come-here motion.

"I care."

"Give me." He reached for her foot and held on even when she tried to pull away. He stripped off her ankle sock and kneaded her sole with his thumb. Instantly, she stopped fighting him.

"Oh, my gosh, that hurts so good." She moaned.

"Hold on, darling, we're just getting started."

Darling? Had he just called her darling? Wyatt cringed, afraid she'd think it was a cheesy endearment, but she was lying flat on her back, her eyes closed, a dreamy smile on her face. She was getting into it. Good, good.

After a few minutes he moved to the other foot and the only sounds were the breeze rustling through the palm trees and Kiara's gentle breathing. He smiled. He'd done it. He'd gotten her to relax completely.

In fact, she was so relaxed she'd fallen asleep.

Wyatt felt a sweet tugging sensation in the center of his chest. A sensation that was at once foreign and welcome. This was his kind of day, easy, lazy and slow-paced. And he'd gotten her to share it with him.

He stretched out beside her, propped up on one elbow, and gazed down at her, watching her sleep. Her chest rose and fell in a smooth, even rhythm. Her eyes were closed so he reached over to remove her glasses.

Without the barrier of her glasses, she appeared incredibly young and vulnerable. It shocked him, the fact that he wanted to just stare and stare and stare at her. He couldn't get enough of looking at her.

She smiled in her sleep and the sight of it kicked him in the gut.

He wished they were in Greece. He'd love to show her his home. Take her around to all his favorite spots. She'd bloom there. Away from her family and responsibility. Away from the winery.

The idea of it made him feel excited in a way he hadn't in a very long time. Why? What was so compelling about Kiara? Why was she always on his mind? Why, for the most part, had he given up spying on her and started truly to be her intern?

Speaking of which, he'd promised his brothers he'd check in with them this weekend.

He got up from the pallet and left her sleeping, then walked to the edge of the water where the sailboat was anchored, pulled out his cell phone and gave his brothers a call.

"So what have you found out?" Scott asked.

Wyatt thought of the problems Kiara had been having with the grapes. He could tell his brothers about that, or he could just keep his mouth shut. "Not much."

"Some spy you are."

"C'mon," Wyatt coaxed. "I've haven't even been here a month. What were you expecting?"

"The secret to why Bella Notte's wines are kicking our ass."

"Honestly," Wyatt said. "I think it's Idyll."

"What?"

"There's something magical about this island." Wyatt turned and glanced back up the hill to where he'd left Kiara sleeping.

"What are you talking about?"

"It's this earth. This place. I believe the only way you could replicate Bella Notte's results is to buy some land here and plant your own vineyard."

Scott snorted. "Seriously, little brother? That's the best you can do?"

"It's the only explanation I can come up with." That and Kiara's supreme devotion to winemaking. He'd never seen anyone with her level of commitment. And the wine industry was chock-full of dedicated vintners, so that was saying something.

"Her wine Decadent Midnight is going to beat you boys at the Best of the Best and there's nothing you can do to change that."

"The hell you say," Scott snapped. "There's always something you can do to kneecap the competition."

"You are not going to kneecap her," Wyatt growled. "This is a tiny, family-owned winery. These people are just trying to get by."

"Yeah, by dethroning us."

"That's nothing but DeSalme ego talking." Wyatt splayed a hand to the nape of his neck, anger surging through him.

He wasn't easy to anger. In fact, he hardly ever got

mad. But Scott was getting on his last nerve. "There's no way Bella Notte could be serious competition. Yes, they might win awards and take a small bite out of our dessert-wine market share, but they have no goals beyond providing a good living for their family. They have practically no distribution. All Kiara wants is to make quality wine and ensure that the winery survives for future generations. You should see her. She's so passionate about wine. Her face lights up and she—"

"Ha. I'll be damned," Scott said, disbelief in his voice.

"What is it?"

Scott hooted. "I never thought this day would come. Wait until I tell Eric."

"What are you talking about?"

"You. You've fallen in love with Kiara Romano."

"I have not," Wyatt denied hotly.

"Hey, Eric." He heard Scott shout. "Guess what? Wyatt's in love."

"I'm not in love." Irritation welled up in him and he thought of all the times his brothers had teased him when he was a kid. It had been tough growing up with two older brothers who were always pulling pranks on him. He'd learned that the best way to deal with them was never let them see him sweat. He'd developed the survival skill of allowing everything to roll smoothly off his back. He reminded himself of that lesson now. Scott was simply trying to get a rise out of him. Well, he wasn't going to let that happen. If Scott wanted to tease, he would play along.

"Wyatt and Kiara sitting in a tree…"

"Mature. Real mature, Scott."

"K.I.S.S.I.N.G."

"Okay, yeah, you got me dead to rights. I'm truly, madly deeply in love with Kiara Romano. I admit it. Happy now?"

"All right," Scott conceded. "You might not be in love with her—because frankly, I can't see you giving up your Lamborghini women for some plain-jane grape farmer—but you do admire her."

Wyatt had to bite his tongue to keep from jumping on Scott for calling Kiara "Plain-jane." He did not want to stir the pot. "I gotta go," he said.

"Call next week and keep us posted. In the meantime, keep your pants zipped. If you're this crazy about her now, I'd hate to see what happens if you were to sleep with her."

"I'm hanging up now." He punched the off button, pocketed his phone and turned around to find Kiara standing behind him, staring him straight in the eyes, a very odd expression on her face.

Panic swept over him.

Just how long had she been standing there?

HAD KIARA HEARD Wyatt correctly? Had he just told someone on the other end of the phone that he was in love with *her?*

Her heart reeled crazily in her chest. But how could that be? They'd only known each other a few weeks. Granted they had great chemistry and things were moving quickly toward a sexual liaison—she had brought a condom with her.

But love? No way. No how. She wasn't ready for anything like that. Didn't know if she would ever be ready to fall in love with a man like Wyatt. Falling heedlessly

in love flew in the face of everything she stood for—
logic, coolheadedness, emotional strength.

But she couldn't deny the hot rush of excitement
coursing through her blood. She wanted Wyatt.

It's just lust. Chemistry, sex. Nothing more.

He stared at her sheepishly, but neither one of them
made a move or said anything. Finally, after a long
moment, he said, "That was just… I was talking to…
my brothers."

"Oh," she said mildly, belying the rich gallop of her
pulse.

"Did you have a nice nap?"

"Yes," she said. "I feel a bit embarrassed falling
asleep on you like that."

"You needed the rest."

"So," she said, deciding to ignore what she'd over-
heard. She definitely could have been mistaken about
what he'd said. She didn't want to assume anything. No
need to freak out.

Wyatt was walking away, putting distance between
them. "Yes?"

"What's next on the agenda?" She laced her fingers
together, a pitiful defense against the doubt assailing
her.

"I thought that we could go for a walk. There are
supposed to be some caves on this island. If you're up
for exploring them?"

"There *are* caves on the island," she said.

"Have you been there before?"

"Not since I was a kid."

"Do you want to find them? Or is that lame?"

"Not lame," she said, but not sure she wanted to be
with him in a dark, confined place. Not sure she could

trust herself alone with him in such a situation. "I'd love to."

He reached out and took her hand.

Her galloping pulse came to one momentous halt, then jump-started again with a wild, irregular rhythm. This wasn't normal. Something was wrong with her. She felt dizzy and off-balance and she wasn't thinking about work or wine.

Why wasn't she thinking about wine?

Why? Because the man peering deeply into her eyes had robbed her of all rational thought.

He held on to her hand and she had no inclination to take it away. They walked up the hill together, past their blanket and picnic basket. The caves weren't far. In the middle of the week like this, the atoll was deserted. No tourists hanging around. The locals were all working. They had the place to themselves.

More danger.

It took less than ten minutes to get to the caves. They held hands the whole way. It felt so intimate, this casual act of affection.

They reached the mouth of the caves. There was a sign-in book inside a protective wooden box so the park rangers knew to come looking for them if they didn't return in a timely manner.

Wyatt let go of her hand long enough to sign them in, then reached for her hand and drew her into the darkened cave. He pulled a flashlight from his pocket and flicked it on. Inside it smelled damp and musty. A small rivulet of water ran through the middle of the cave. There were two walking paths, one on either side of the water. Wyatt went first. Kiara felt as if she were back in high school, coming to make out with her date, even though she'd never done such a thing. In high school, she'd been in the honor society, too busy getting good grades to do anything so daring.

"You know," she said. "The Idyll winery owners used these caves to hide their bottles during prohibition."

"We're not supposed to be talking business today," Wyatt reminded her.

The stalactites overhead dripped water into the rivulet with a soft plunking noise.

"This isn't about work," she said. "This is history."

"It's borderline work."

"Can you imagine what it was like living back then?"

"When wine was outlawed? A dark day in history."

"It almost killed wine-making on Idyll. It probably would have if we hadn't been so isolated. If they hadn't had these caves to store the bottles in."

Names had been carved into the cave walls. Tourists leaving their marks. Lovers etching their names, proclaiming their love. Schoolkids showing off for each other. Defacing the cave was an odd tradition she didn't approve of, but she couldn't deny there was a sense of history seeing the names of people who had come before them. People just like them who had worked and played and fallen in love.

Watch it, Kiara, you're in danger of sounding whimsical.

No one had ever accused her of being whimsical, and yet here she was thinking whimsical thoughts. It was all Wyatt's fault. Until he had shown up, she'd had her head screwed firmly onto her shoulders.

Once they were out of sight of the opening and the only light was from the thin flashlight beam, Wyatt stopped.

"What is it?" Kiara whispered.

"This."

He flicked off the flashlight. Kiara gasped at the sudden darkness. Excitement lifted goose bumps on her arms. The complete darkness was both scary and exhilarating.

Wyatt's arms went around her. He pulled her up tight against his chest.

Kiara did not protest. Her whole body was alive. Tense with anticipation. She licked her lips. Waited.

His kiss came slowly, in inches. First his mouth was on her cheek. Just resting there. Then he slid his lips toward hers. Her body tightened in response, every part of her growing taut from her nipples to her feminine core.

He found her mouth and pressed his lips to hers. Lightly. No rush. No pressure. Simply there.

In the blackness of the cave all visual sense was gone. Only sound, touch, taste and smell existed. His lively scent was a delightful contrast to the dankness of the cave. The sound of his breathing a brilliant accompaniment to the plunk, plunk, plunk of water sliding down the cave walls. His taste sweet as Decadent Midnight.

Her fingers found his chin in the darkness, slid up his jaw to cradle the back of his head in her palm.

Her rib cage was pressed flush against Wyatt's chest and she could feel his hardness straining against his jeans, poking audaciously into her side. Her own desire ramped skyward.

The palm of his hand was pressed against her butt. She ached to have his skin against hers. Yearned to feel his palm playfully swat her fanny.

His fingers went to the zipper of her denim shorts

and she did not stop him. He kissed her, teased her bottom lip up between his teeth. She moaned softly into his mouth.

He eased his hand past the open zipper, down the waistband of her panties.

Her breath slipped threadily past her teeth, he was right where she wanted him to be, yes, yes. His kisses started an inferno inside her and his fingers, oh! His fingers! His wicked, wicked fingers.

Her body was so slick for him. When he slipped an index finger inside her, she let out a soft mewling noise.

Wyatt's mouth crushed hers—hungry, demanding, fast. Ha! She wasn't the only one who had trouble slowing down.

His tongue thrust past her teeth, discerning, exploring, then teasing and savoring, and all the while his finger was buried inside her.

She wriggled against his hand, wanting more pressure. His other hand stroked her nipple through her T-shirt until it was stiff and sensitive.

Their raspy breathing echoed off the cave walls, making it sound as though there were other people in the cave with them. That escalated her excitement.

Her shorts where slipping down her hips and the next thing she knew they were around her ankles. With a soft growl, Wyatt lightly bit the side of neck, sending fresh shivers spiriting down her nerve endings.

His biceps bunched as he held her. She could feel his muscles flex. He pressed her back to the cave wall. In the pitch black she reached for him, found his head level with her breast, one palm skimming up underneath her shoulder, his other palm spread against the curls between her thighs, his index finger still inside her, gently stroking. Her panties slipped down to join her denim shorts around her ankles. She raised her arms over her head, grasped hold of the rough, damp cave wall as Wyatt pressed his hot mouth to her cool belly.

Kiara writhed against him.

The scent of her womanhood rose in the darkness. The deep musky aroma around her, the smell of her feminine power lifting her to a fever pitch. She felt like the ancient goddess of wine and this man kneeling before her worshipped her. It was a startling fantasy for a woman who didn't put much emphasis on such things.

"Kiara, you are so beautiful."

"You can't even see me."

"I can feel you all around me."

The smells and sensations inundated her. The subterranean cool of the cave. The rich aroma of her own body. The sound of the water dripping into water pools. Primal. Basic. Raw.

Kiara was barely breathing. Wyatt's tongue was trekking a purposeful path down her belly, going lower and lower. How utterly erotic. Her fingers found his hair, tangled in the thick strands. She pressed her back solidly against the porous rock wall behind her as if she was glued to it.

"Spread your legs," he said.

"Wh—" She moistened her lips. "What are you going to do?"

His laughter was devilish. "What do you think?"

"I…I don't know if I like that."

"What? No one had ever gone down on you before?"

"No," she whispered.

"Oh, you poor, poor, darling. We're going to fix that

oversight right now." Then his mouth was there, where his hand had been.

This was great, this was wonderful, this was scary. She issued a prayer, thanking the heavens for sending her a man with such an accomplished tongue. A bit of embarrassment was thrown in, but his mouth soon whisked away those worries.

His tongue found her most sensitive hood. Her tender flesh bloomed and he sucked with inexorable gentleness, stirring her thick pleasure.

"Wyatt," she murmured restlessly, thrashing her head against the wall. "Wyatt."

She clung to his hair, savoring the wild, sensory ride, letting loose for once, not holding back. His touch was incredible and she was unprepared for her body's flammable reaction. His tongue laved and caressed her. She ached and trembled. Craved and cried out. Her skin sung an endless song. Her heart wept with happy gratitude.

Thank you, thank you, thank you.

Carefully, his masterful mouth manipulated her taut feminine peak until it was stiff and throbbing. She whispered and moaned, laughed and sighed, barely able to tolerate the exquisiteness of it all.

"Ooh, ooh, Wy—*att*."

"That's it. Call for me, darling."

She clung to him, digging her fingers into his shoulder muscles. So close, so close, so ready to climax. She was dripping wet for him, soaked to the core. She was afire, alive, burning with need for him. She was trapped in the sensation.

His tongue waltzed and tangoed, flicked and tickled. The wet, slippery glide was unbelievable. His fingers were back, teasing her molten center. She rocked into him, held his head against her pelvis, begged for more, more, more, but even as she did, the dual motions of fingers and tongue were more than she could bear.

"Please, please, please."

Ever so lightly, he barely touched his teeth to her pulsating hood and that was it.

Her control shattered into a million brilliant pieces and dropped blindly into the orgasmic abyss.

10

*Finish: How long the flavor
lasts in the mouth.*

ALL THE WAY back to Idyll Wyatt mentally chastised
himself. The red-hot desire that burned so out of control whenever he was around Kiara unsettled him. He
thought of the song "Every Which Way But Loose"
again. He'd thought of it the first time he'd laid eyes
on Kiara. Without even trying, she did indeed turn him
every which way but loose.

The thing of it was, he didn't want her to let him
loose. He wanted her to grab hold of him and hold on
with both hands for dear life. Forever and ever. Amen.

But he couldn't tell her that.

She was sitting up front, her face turned into the
wind, her auburn curls flowing out behind her like
flames. The late-afternoon sun cast her features in an
ethereal glow. How had he ever thought her frumpy?
He must have been off his rocker. She was the most supreme of goddesses.

That he couldn't have.

Not until he came clean about who he was, and once she found out who he was, she'd hate him.

Because he was her enemy.

KIARA DANCED INTO her apartment feeling better than she'd felt in…well, *honestly*…had she ever felt this good?

Wyatt had kissed her on the porch. She'd invited him in, but he'd told her that she needed her rest. She was still recuperating from her cold and shouldn't overdo it.

"Too late." She'd grinned. He'd given her a heck of a workout in that cave.

"Besides," he said, "tomorrow is the first night of the full moon and Maurice said the place gets crazy for those three days in June. He wants the interns up extra early to get ready for the influx of tourists."

"Technically, the full moon is only one second long," she said. "But that doesn't play well in romance land, so around here, we call it a full moon as along as it looks pretty full to the naked eye. We sell more wine in those three days alone than we do throughout the entire rest of the month. It's madness and I can't believe I forgot that tomorrow is the first day."

"You've had other things on your mind." He grinned.

"Your fault. You know," she said, "I should put you back in the lab and send Lauren to the vineyards."

"That wouldn't be fair to Lauren," he said.

"You're a better assistant."

"Why, thank you." He kissed her forehead, his lips leaving a hot little brand on her skin. "Good night and get some sleep."

Then he turned in the twilight to walk to the interns'

quarters, the most wistful expression she'd ever seen on his face. She'd almost called to him and told him the hell with her cold and their busiest days of the year, and to get in her bed now. But she didn't. She needed some time alone to process what was unfolding between them and how she felt about it.

So she closed the door, turned on her MP3 player and humming to the Black Keys's "Too Afraid to Love You," she twirled around the room.

Felix greeted her by butting his fuzzy head against her calf and twining around her legs. She picked him up, stroked his chin. "My bad boy now tamed."

He meowed.

"Oh, you disagree, huh? Still have some spunk in you yet? I suppose no bad boy is ever totally reformed."

Felix wriggled to get down and she let him go.

She thought of Wyatt and his wicked tongue. There was some bad-boy action she never wanted to see reformed. Oh, gosh, had she actually let him do that to her? Grinning, she covered her face with her hands.

Were they actually embarking on a wild fling? She could handle that. She just needed to know that's what it was. She didn't want to get her hopes up because she could see herself falling in love with him if she wasn't careful.

The Black Keys announced that they were too afraid to love.

Apparently it was epidemic.

Okay, she had to be reasonable. This feeling was lust. Pure and simple. Well, maybe not so simple, but it was physical, hormone-fueled biology. Understandable.

Why then did she have a sudden urge to raid her

cousins' storybook collection for a copy of *Cinderella* or *Snow White* or any of those other fairy-tale princess stories she'd eschewed as a six-year-old?

So where did they go from here? Who made the next move? Should she let him? Would it be too bold if she did it? This was crazy-making.

Deep breath. Chill. You don't have to label it right now. No expectations. Take it as it comes. Concentrate.

The Best of the Best Award was coming up on July first, a kick-off to the long holiday weekend just three days away. Three hectic days filled with Full Moon in Juners descending on Idyll. She'd focus on getting ready for that and then, after Bella Notte won the competition, she'd let things between her and Wyatt take their natural course.

Satisfied with her plan, Kiara went to bed and quickly fell into a deep sleep filled with sexy dreams of a good-looking dark-eyed man who knew how to do incredibly delightful things with his awesome tongue.

WHILE KIARA SLEPT like a baby, Wyatt paced the grounds outside the dormitories. What was he going to do? He was torn, trying to think of the best way to confess.

First you have to call Scott and Eric in their Sonoma, California, offices and tell them that you're out.

He checked his watch. It was almost midnight. He didn't care. He couldn't sleep until he settled this. Eric might still be up. He was a night owl like Wyatt. He yanked the cell phone from his pocket and punched the speed dial for his brother.

"Yo!"

"You still up?"

"I'm answering the phone, aren't I? What's up baby brother? You got any juicy info for us?"

"Yeah, I'm quitting."

"What?"

"You heard me."

"Dammit, you're calling a default?" Eric said. "I owe Scott a hundred bucks. I swore you wouldn't cross-face us."

"I'm not cross-facing you," Wyatt said, using the wrestling term in order to communicate with his brother. The guy was still hung up on his college victories. "I'm escaping."

In wrestling terms, *escape* was used to indicate when a bottom man frees himself from the top man's control, coming out of the bottom position. Well, he'd been in the bottom position for thirty-one years and he was done.

"Give Scott the message, will you?"

"He's going to be really disappointed."

"Sorry," Wyatt said, "I've made good my escape."

"So when you come to the Best of the Best Award—"

"I'll be on Bella Notte's side."

"Dude, that's as foul as a full Nelson."

"You ought to know. You pulled them on me often enough." Just like that, Wyatt had thrown his lot in with David against Goliath.

The first part of his mission was over. Now for the hardest part. Coming clean to Kiara.

The last day of the full moon fell on June thirtieth. The day before the Best of the Best Award in Sonoma. He'd tell her then. He'd take her to the top of Twin Hearts, ply her with Decadent Midnight and then tell her the truth about who he was.

THE NEXT THREE days were totally chaotic. The parking lot at Bella Notte was filled to overflowing. Cash registers rang constantly. Bicycles built for two clogged the road up to Twin Hearts bluff. Everyone at Bella Notte was pressed into service.

Everywhere Wyatt looked there were lovers, both young and old, holding hands, picnicking in fields, wandering through the vineyards, take the winery tours. It was just as crowded in Idyll when he went into the village for supplies.

Things didn't start to wind down at Bella Notte until the last evening of the full moon. The winery closed at five to the general public, but the road outside was still lined with cars on their way up to the peak. He had to hand it to the Romanos, their romantic legend certainly lit a fire in people's hearts.

Feeling more than a bit nervous, Wyatt approached Kiara as they finished cleaned up the tasting room after the day's traffic.

"There's something I need to talk to you about," he said.

She gathered up wineglasses and put them on a tray. "I'm listening."

"Somewhere private."

"This is private." She waved a hand at the empty room.

Wyatt shook his head. "A Romano or an intern could stroll in here at any time."

Kiara's brow furrowed. "This sounds serious."

"Could you just indulge me?"

A smile tilted her lips. "Oh, I get it. This is code for let's go make out. I know we've been swamped from dawn to twilight for the last three days and haven't had a chance to talk."

"You got me," Wyatt admitted. Anything to get her to leave with him. He had to tell her who he was and what he was up to. He couldn't let her get to Sonoma without spilling his guts. He couldn't handle the guilt of it anymore. Didn't want to handle the guilt. Their relationship couldn't move to the next level until she knew who he really was.

Ha! After you tell her who you are, do you really think there's going to be a next level? Be real, DeSalme.

"It's a beautiful night at Bella Notte. We only have a few weeks left together."

A sad expression came into her eyes. An expression that matched the heavy feeling settling into the pit of his stomach. He was so afraid he was going to lose her.

Don't tell her.

He had to tell her. He should have told her before now.

If you tell her, she's going to throw you out.

"Let's go up to Twin Hearts," he muttered.

"On a full moon? In June." She shook her head. "No way."

"Because of the legend."

"Yes, because of the legend that if you and your sweetheart share a bottle of Belle Notte wine beneath a full moon in June at Twin Hearts, you will be together forever. Throngs of tourists will be up there waiting for some silly myth to strike them. It's nuts."

"If you don't believe in the myth, then what are you so afraid of?"

"I'm not afraid. Who says I'm afraid?"

"Prove you're not afraid. Let's go."

"Nothing is going to happen."

He reached out a hand to caress her and she sank against him. He loved how she responded to his touch. "You mean nothing that doesn't normally happen when the two of us get together."

"Nothing is normal with you Wyatt," she purred.

"Right back at you, Kiara."

She kissed his throat. "Forget Twin Hearts. Let's make love right here. We'll lock the doors."

He chuckled. "I can't believe how much you've changed. Four weeks ago you wouldn't have dreamed of using the tasting room as a rendezvous spot."

"True," she admitted, "but you have taught me the value of recharging my batteries."

"So let's take things one step further. I pushed you from your comfort zone and look how much fun you've been having. Not only how much fun you've been having, but how much more productive you are. Let's push some more. Come on, let's go up to Twin Hearts."

She looked up into his eyes. "Wyatt, I hope you aren't expecting anything more from this relationship than I'm able to give."

He made a derisive noise, but inside he felt sick. "No, no, of course not. My goal is to help you."

"Help me? How's that?"

"Look how you let the myth control your life."

"The myth doesn't control my life," she argued.

"Then prove it. Go to the peak with me."

"Okay, fine," she said. "I'll go. I'll prove it's nothing but a crazy myth. But I have to be home early. Tomorrow is the Best of the Best Award in Sonoma."

"No problem."

"Let me finish up here and I'll meet you in the parking lot in thirty minutes."

KIARA COULDN'T BELIEVE she'd agreed to go to the peak with Wyatt. She'd spent her adult life avoiding this very scenario.

But she had to admit that Wyatt made a good point. By avoiding Twin Hearts, she was letting the legend control her life just as surely as the romantics allowed it to control theirs. So even though it made her uneasy, she agreed to go.

They took a Bella Notte van, but ended up having to park half a mile away on the side of the bluff because the parking lot was jam-packed.

"I told you," Kiara said. "It gets crazy around here on the full moon in June. The peak is littered with lovers. It's not going to be the least bit private."

"We're here in defiance, remember?" Wyatt reached out to squeeze her hand. "To prove there's no such thing as the Romano myth. Besides, Maurice told me the secret spot that's off-limits to tourist."

"You told Maurice you were bringing me up here!"

"Course not. I just asked where the Romanos go for their romantic full-moon liaisons. He told me where the Romano property line ends and public access begins." He reached into the backseat for the blanket and a brown paper bag.

"You brought wine!"

"We can't disprove the myth if we didn't follow it to the letter."

"It makes me nervous."

"If it's only a myth you have nothing to worry about,

right?" He was too damned convincing with his adorable smile and winsome eyes.

Yes, all right, so why did she feel so vulnerable? Hope, that damnable thing, was nibbling around the edges of her mind. The romantic Romano soul clashing with Kiara's scientific mind. It wasn't until they were halfway up the bluff, picking their way past picnickers feeding each other, opening bottles of Decadent Midnight, kissing under the bright light of the full moon, that she realized part of her secretly wanted to believe it was all true.

"There's no such thing as Santa Claus," she muttered under her breath like a child whistling in the dark to prove she's not afraid of it.

"Maybe not," Wyatt whispered. "But there *is* the spirit of Christmas."

"All these people." She swept her hand at the blankets and lovers spread out across the field. "If they end up staying together for the rest of their lives, it's just a self-fulfilling prophecy. It's got nothing to do with Idyll or bottles of wine or a full moon."

"What's wrong with that? I think it's amazing how this island and your family gives so many people hope for a lasting relationship."

It was a very noble thought. She had to admit that.

"What is it that you're afraid of, Kiara?" Wyatt said. "Everyone in your family is living the myth. They're all happily married."

"That's a myth too. No one is happily married all the time. Like when my dad was diagnosed with cancer. It was incredibly heart-breaking to see my parents go through that. They loved each other so much that the thought of losing each other tore them apart. Love makes you weak."

"Whoa." Wyatt backed up, angled his head and stared at her in the moonlight. "I get it now."

Kiara wrinkled her nose in irritation. "What is it that you think you get?"

"You're afraid of the power of that kind of love. You think it would obscure your objectivity."

"It would, but that's not the reason I don't believe. I don't believe it because it's not true. Love is nothing more than body chemistry. It makes people…" She paused, made air quotes with her fingers. "…fall in love."

"What's wrong with that?"

"The chemicals fade. Time passes."

"The relationship cements."

"And what does cement do but drag you down?"

"You really are terrified of falling in love."

"You're not?"

"Not anymore." They were at the very top of the peak now. There was a wooden fence marking the edge of the Romano land. There was a Private Property sign posted.

"This way," she said, ducking under the fence and pulling Wyatt along with her.

They walked until they could no longer hear the conversations of the other people on the bluff.

"How about here?" Kiara said stopping in a grove of olive trees.

The full moon was high in the sky, casting a silvery glow over everything. It filtered through the olive trees, bathing Wyatt's face in shadow. He nodded and spread out the blanket.

Kiara lay down on the blanket beside him, remembering what had happened the last time they'd lain on a blanket together. "Okay, let's do this myth-busting thing. Open up the wine."

"You sure? You don't have to do this if you don't want to."

"I'm here. Might as well take the plunge."

He uncorked the wine, then looked at her. "What if the myth is true? Would you still want to take the plunge?"

"We barely know each other."

He reached out and tapped her heart with his index finger. "You know."

That made her suck in a deep breath. "Are you saying follow my instincts?"

"Animals follow their instincts. That's pretty scientific." He took a sip from the wine, then passed the bottle to her.

"There's really no way other than instinct." She took a drink, passed it back as if they were taking some kind of bizarre communion.

"Just go with it."

"That could be emotion. There's a big difference between emotion and instinct."

"Man is an emotional being." He took another drink, passed the bottle again.

"True enough, but emotions aren't logical."

"Doesn't stop people from feeling them."

Kiara took her second drink. Then reached for the cork on the blanket. "There," she said. "It's done. Feel any different?"

The moon was at its zenith now. Fat and round, the color of Swiss cheese.

"Yep."

"How's that?"

"I want you ten times more than I wanted you before we drank the wine."

"Now is that the moon, or the alcohol taking?"

"Neither," he said leaning in close. "It's one-hundred-percent Kiara."

He held out his arm and she just rolled into his embrace, the smell of wine and summer love in the air. He brought her snug against his chest and time slowed to this one perfect moment under the full moon in June with the man who made her feel more alive than she'd ever felt.

She heard her heart pounding, felt his beat a corresponding rhythm through the material of his shirt. She planted a kiss on his neck, traveled up to find his earlobe. His familiar scent filled her nostril, reached down and caressed her lungs.

Wyatt.

She wasn't sure how much of this feeling she could stand. It was too strong, too wild, too un-Kiara-like. She was accustomed to being confident and in charge. Being with Wyatt was like taking a bulldozer to the elaborate sand castle you'd spent fifteen hours building on the beach.

But oh, how she wanted him. And that's what scared her most of all. This desire—burning, raging, out of control. She knew for certain this feeling was what she'd been avoiding. Wyatt made her feel *real*. And she simply didn't know what to do about it. He could break her so easily. Shatter her heart clean in two.

She saw a shadow of something in his eyes. Where do we go from here? Is it time? Is it right? Should we just take a leap of faith and jump? How do we keep from hurting each other? The questions poured in on her, but she did not speak her doubts aloud.

Wyatt was spur of the moment, free as the wind. He didn't have the restriction of family.

He reached out and took off her glasses, then removed his own and set them to one side. Then he kissed her. Slow and sweet.

Kiara felt the tingle all the way to her toes. He made her feel exposed, raw. He was dangerous. She was accustomed to being strong, in control, in charge. With one well-placed kiss on top of Twin Hearts, he took it all away.

His teeth nibbled her earlobe and he tightened his grip. "Do you like that?"

She whimpered. "Yes."

"Mmm, good to know. I love how you smell, the way you taste, salty, yet sweet. That's the way of you, Kiara, tart-tongued at times, but it's only to hide that tender heart."

He skimmed his hands up underneath her blouse, his palms slipping over skin. His fingers skated around to unhook her bra and the next thing she knew it was off her, flung across the blanket.

Wyatt took her breath, and her wandering thoughts, when he ensnared her lips with his hot, wet mouth and sucked her skin. Radiant heat mushroomed outward, across her shoulders, headed pell-mell for her breasts.

Her pulse leaped, bounded. Her nipples tightened. She reveled into the luxury of his embrace and took a deep breath. She inhaled the pure essence of Wyatt.

He lowered his sultry lids halfway. Lust for her burned in his eyes, stiffening his erection.

"Do you want me to stop now?" he whispered. "Have we gone too far? Are you out of your comfort zone?"

She could back out. End this here. "I'm comfortable."

He felt so good. She felt good. What he was doing felt wonderful. Everything about this man made her want to beg for him.

Take me, take what you want, leave me scorched to the ground, bare and burned and savagely sated.

"What's your pleasure?" he whispered.

"You," she whispered back. "I want you."

He nibbled her throbbing pulse points. The sensation sent aching spikes of awareness flooding her entire body. She moaned softly.

His thumbs brushed lazily against her nipples, tightened the already stiff peaks, driving her crazy. Her breath hung up somewhere between her lungs and her throat. No air, just the smell of Wyatt.

The moon was so bright, so intense it felt as if it was shining just for them. She thought of the generations of Romanos who'd come up here, drunk wine, made love, vowed their undying love. She and Wyatt were part of history, part of tradition. A tradition she'd resisted even though she did not know why.

Tenderly, they undressed each other and shared slow, soft, wet kisses. They were in their own utopia, just the two of them, blissed out on each other. Needing nothing, no one but themselves. Their own little world.

Her hands were on the hem of his T-shirt, dragging it up and over his head. Bye-bye, T-shirt. Hello, hard-muscled man. She whistled in a breath, traced shaky fingers over his chest.

His hands wrestled with her dress, undid the buttons, tugged it from her body.

Then they were naked, pressed skin to skin, chest to breast. A raw, nagging twinge bloomed between her thighs. Her hands were cold against his heated belly.

Things were advancing, getting heavy. Doubts crept in. She'd wanted this. Dreamed of this for weeks. What if she couldn't please him? What if she was lousy in bed—er, blanket on the ground?

"Stop it," he chided.

"Stop what?"

"Thinking. You're thinking too much."

"How do you know?"

"You always think too much."

"*Always* is a broad generalization."

"Okay, you think too much ninety percent of the time."

"Maybe you don't think enough."

"That's highly possible," he said amicably. "But just stay here with me in the moment. We'll never have this time again."

He was right. He was so good at making her appreciate what was right in front of her. She loved him for that. And so many other things.

Love.

Okay, she'd admit it. She was falling in love with him. She should be scared, right? But instead…well, she felt free. She wasn't ready to tell him yet. Wasn't ready to weigh the implications of what this meant. Especially in regard to the myth they were supposed to be busting, but she couldn't deny what she was feeling any longer. She'd tried to hide it from herself, but it was a useless exercise. She felt what she felt.

Wyatt.

She reached up to trace his cheek with her fingers

and he peered deeply into her eyes. He looked up at her in total awe. The light in his eyes shook her very soul. The pleasure of his words, the expression of pure gratitude on his face toasted her skin, warmed her heart. He pressed his cheek against her belly, blew lightly across her skin. Goose bumps cropped up, making her giggle.

"I love to hear you laugh. It's the best sound in the world."

"You have a much better laugh."

"Yours is worth more because you don't use it as often."

"Interesting point of view."

They lay down on the blanket, then their hands got busy exploring. They strummed and played. Tongues and teeth. Lips and noses. Tickles and feather-light touches.

He kissed the pulses under her chin and it made her clit throb. She nibbled the sensitive skin on the underside of his arm and he shuddered. He licked the back of her knee. She ran her tongue over his collarbone.

They teased and stroked, kneaded and caressed until they had both reached a frantic pitch, perspiring, breathing heavily, aching to the bone for release.

His thumbs brushed her nipples and she let out a hungry moan. Had she ever felt a pleasure this delicious?

She was overpowered, overwhelmed, overcome, over-everything. "I've gotta have you or lose my mind," she rasped.

"C'mere," he said and pulled her on top of him so that she was straddling his waist.

She was ready and slick and slid easily over his rock-hard shaft, merging her body with his.

"Kiara." He breathed out a heavy sigh as she sank onto him.

She glanced down at him. The big man underneath. She was in control. He was letting her have her way and he was staring at her with adoring eyes.

Now, now, gotta have him. Can't wait, can't stop, can't think, can't breathe.

She moved over him. Wyatt groaned. She slid back and forth over his lean, hard-muscled body. Friction hardened his shaft, heated her.

He threw his head back, his dark hair spilling over the blanket, exposed throat gone stark-white in the full moonlight. She rocked against him, gliding and rolling in a sweet rhythm.

Wyatt raised his head, pulled her down lower so he could capture one of her pert nipples with his mouth and gently tug at her with an erotic suction.

While he was doing that, she reached down to cup his balls in her palm with the lightest of pressure. He jerked, groaned. "You keep that up, this will be over in no time."

The night breeze cooled their heated skin. The full moon bathed in them in a splash of vineyard light. The olive-tree branches creaked.

He rocked his hips in time to her movements. She stared into his face, got lost in his chocolate eyes. She quickened the pace, sliding up, then falling back, riding the length of him again and again.

"My turn to be in control now," he said, then grasped her around the waist and flipped her over while they stayed connected.

In and out. He moved slow and sure. Their bodies

undulating as he kissed her. Their souls tied, bound, connected.

Every nerve in her body was alive, on edge.

His movements quickened. From slow to staccato, thrusting into her deeper, higher, faster. He was on fire. A wild man. But no wilder than she. He pushed her legs up over her head, opening her wide, entering her as deeply as possible, pounding her hard.

"More," she cried. "More. Harder, faster."

Slow and leisurely was over. He was moving at her speed now, pumping into her with vigorous intensity.

They spun, twisted, turned, lost in the whirl of magic and passion, caught up in mythology, lore and the reckless legend of love.

She finally let go when the orgasm overtook her. His noises were as rough and loud as her own. Their bodies jerked in unison. And as they came they cried each other's names over and over. They clung together, thanks to the moon and mist and decadent midnight.

11

Tears: A poetic reference to the drips of wine left on the side of a wine glass after it has been swirled.

WHEN KIARA AWOKE, the moon had disappeared and the faint fingers of sunrise had begun to tickle the eastern horizon. Where was she? What had she done?

She jolted to a sitting position, raising a hand in a pathetic attempt to cover her nudity. Wyatt lay stretched out beside her, sleeping soundly.

The bottle of Decadent Midnight lay on the ground.

The implications of what they'd done struck her hard. She wasn't ready for this. Last night she'd been swept away. The light of day—

The Best of the Best Award! It was today. In Sonoma. An hour's ride by ferry and then a good three-and-half-hour drive. The judging was at 2:00 p.m. but the contestants had to check in by noon.

And it was…she glanced at her watch.

Five o'clock. She gritted her teeth at the silly watch, then guessed it really must be close to 5:00 a.m. She

needed to get moving, get back to Bella Notte, get the
wine loaded and get to Sonoma by noon.

She got dressed, uncertain what to do about Wyatt.
She wasn't ready to talk to him. She needed to process
her own feelings first. Her mind raced ninety miles an
hour and none of her thoughts were making much sense.
Only one thing came through loud and clear:

Get to Sonoma.

She stuck her glasses on her face and took one last
look at him. He was indeed magnificent. Her heart
clutched. Was she in love with him? For so long she'd
denied such a thing was possible and now she was in
the middle of it.

Get to Sonoma.

Yes. She had to go. Wyatt could wait. The Best of
the Best Award could not.

WYATT AWOKE DAZED and disoriented.

The sun was pushing over the top of the bluff. The
night mist off the water disappeared in the wake of the
sun's rays. The ground was damp and so was the blanket. He shivered, reached for Kiara to pull her closer,
warm her with his body, but he came up with a hand-
ful of air.

Blinking, he sat up, trying to remember what had
happened. They'd drunk the wine. Made love under a
midnight moon in June.

His heart skipped a beat.

They'd fallen asleep.

Now, Kiara was gone. The empty bottle of Decadent
Midnight lay off to one side of the blanket.

Where was Kiara?

Freaking out, probably. Having realized they'd made

love under the very circumstances she'd spent her life avoiding. His chest tightened at the thought of her regretting what they'd done. Wyatt didn't regret it. Not at all. In fact, he was happy.

Happier than he'd ever been in his life.

Well, except for the part where Kiara had taken off.

She was just scared. He didn't blame her. He was scared too. He'd never felt like this about anyone. Hadn't known such intense feelings were possible. He had to find her and calm her down. Reassure her that things hadn't changed between them.

But that was a lie, right? Because things *had* changed. He'd changed. She'd changed him. And he wanted so badly to believe he'd changed her too.

Because if he hadn't, he was out here alone.

In love alone.

Love.

The word hung in his mind; it did not scare him.

That was bizarre enough.

But not only did the realization that he was in love with Kiara not scare him, he relished it. He couldn't wait to tell her.

She's going to think it's just because of the legend. She'd not going to believe it.

Wyatt licked his lips, kneaded his forehead with two fingers. He was going to have to find a way to show her that it was true. Actions always spoke louder than words.

And what of the fact that he'd never gotten around to telling her who he really was? When was he going to sandwich that in there? Before or after he told her that he'd fallen in love with her?

I love you and, oh, by the way, I'm your nemesis.

Wyatt blew out his breath. How had he gotten himself into this mess?

Doesn't matter. Just go find her. You'll think of a way to talk yourself out of this. You always do. Right.

Except his time, he didn't want to be glib or charming, or joke his way into her heart. He wanted to be open and honest. He wanted her to love him at his core, not for the shine he could put on his image.

Then he remembered Sonoma. That's where she was.

Get up! Get moving! Today is the competition. She's got to be frantic trying to get everything loaded up and transported to the mainland. If you really want to prove you love her, get up and go help her.

Wyatt sprang to his feet, grabbed up the blanket, the wine bottle and hurried down the hill.

Twin Hearts looked so compelling in the morning light. Maybe even more compelling than they had looked in moonlight.

All the other couples had disappeared. The parking lot, when he arrived there, lay empty. No vehicles in sight. Kiara had taken the van, gone off and left him.

Why had she left him?

Freak-out. She was having a freak-out.

He could allow her that.

In the meantime, he had a two-mile hike back to Bella Notte. If he ran, he could be there in twenty minutes.

Resolutely, Wyatt took off.

"Hurry, hurry," Kiara urged Maurice. "Let's get the wine loaded up. I've got the bottles we're taking stacked in the lab."

"Calm down," her cousin said. "We've got plenty of

time. We don't have to check in until noon. It's barely six now."

"I want to get there with plenty of time to spare. I want to make sure everything is perfect. I want—" To get out of here before Wyatt wakes up and comes looking for me and wants to talk.

Panicked. She was panicked. Mainly because she was more concerned about the aftermath of spending the night with Wyatt up on Twin Hearts than she was about the competition, and that was distressing.

This was wrong. Very wrong. Nothing mattered more to her than Bella Notte—except for her family—and they were part and parcel of the same thing. She couldn't separate the two.

But now, here she was thinking about the magic of last night. How special it had been, how she could feel herself losing control of a man who was supposed to have been nothing more than a casual summer fling.

Kiara knew it wasn't true. That no matter how much she told herself that Wyatt was just a guy, she knew she was lying to herself.

Lying and hiding from her feelings.

Stop it. Stop thinking about him.

No matter how she chastised herself she could not keep from thinking about how his body felt buried inside hers. How he smelled so rich and sweet like the most sinful chocolates on earth. How she wanted to believe in the legend.

Kiara's intern, Lauren, came from the lab wheeling the crate of wine on a dolly. "You ready to load these?"

"Yes, thank you, you're a sweetheart for helping," Kiara said, grateful.

Maurice assisted Lauren loading up the crates.

Grandmamma came from the house, headed over to the van. "I made cinnamon rolls for your trip."

"Thank you," Kiara said, taking the sack that Grandmamma presented to her.

Lauren turned, went back to the lab.

Grandmamma put her hands on her hips, slanted her head, studied Kiara for a long moment.

"What is it?" Kiara asked, a ripple of alarm sliding through her.

"You look different," Grandmamma said.

Surely what she'd done the night before was not detectable on her face. She'd taken a shower, changed her clothes. Now, she ran a hand through her hair. "No, not different. I'm the same. Exactly the same."

Grandmamma stared as if she didn't believe a word of it. "Where is Wyatt?"

"I don't know. Why should I know? It wasn't my turn to look after him."

Grandmamma and Maurice exchanged a look.

"Last night was the full moon," Grandmamma announced.

"Was it?" Kiara asked, trying to be cool and failing miserably.

"It was."

Maurice and Grandmamma kept staring at her.

"What?" she finally snapped, getting irritated.

A sly smile curled her grandmother's lips. "Nothing," she said. "Enjoy your cinnamon rolls."

She strolled back into the house, but Kiara heard her humming beneath her breath. "Bella Notte." She was humming "Bella Notte."

"My little cousin is finally in love." Maurice laughed.

"I'm not in love," Kiara denied. "Not at all."

"Uh-huh."

"I'm not."

"Where were you last night?"

"That's none of your business. And I'm not in love."

Maurice just laughed louder.

Glowering, Kiara shoved the last crate into the back of the van. Then she climbed inside. "Are you coming or not?"

"Oh," Maurice said. "I wouldn't miss this for the world."

WYATT REACHED BELLA Notte, breathless and sweaty. He'd run the two miles in fifteen minutes with the blanket thrown over his shoulder and the bottle of Decadent Midnight tucked under his arm.

The first person he saw when he arrived was Steve.

Steve stared at him and shook his head. "Dude."

"What is it?"

Steve's eyes widened. "Um…you look a mess."

"Never mind that, where's Kiara?"

"Long gone. She took the morning ferry to the mainland."

Kiara went to the competition without him? He could see her leaving him on the peak. She'd been flustered and embarrassed, maybe even overwhelmed by her feelings. He got that, he was overwhelmed too, but to go off and leave him? Well, his feelings were hurt.

"When's the next ferry?"

"Not for two hours."

He glanced at his watch. He could still make it to the competition by noon.

He tried to call Kiara, but she didn't—or wouldn't—pick up.

"Kiara," he blurted, when it went to voice mail. "Please don't shut me out like this. We have to talk. There's something important I have to tell you. Something I should have told you last night. Call me as soon as you get this. I'm taking the next ferry to the mainland. I'm coming to Sonoma."

He hung up, feeling more guilt than he'd ever felt in his life. Perhaps he should have just told her in the phone message who he was, but he didn't want to break the news to her like that. This was something he needed to tell her in person, face-to-face. He couldn't take the easy way out.

Then a chilling idea occurred to him. What if she'd somehow discovered who he was? That would explain the cold shoulder. But how could she have found out between last night and this morning? Maybe he talked in his sleep? It was a formidable thought. Losing her was a very real possibility.

He went to the lab to kill time until the next ferry. Or at least that's what he told himself. In all honesty, he went there because it was the closest he could come to being with Kiara. He opened the side door and walked in. He sat down at the stool where she had first interviewed him.

Kiara.

He gripped the table. If he lost her, he'd never forgive himself. That's when he noticed the bottle of vinegar sitting on the desk. He got up to put it under the counter. Kiara kept a spotless, well-organized lab. Lauren had probably left it out. When he bent to put the vinegar in the acid cabinet, that's when he saw the 50-cc syringe with the thin-gauge needle in the trash. Now, that was a health hazard. He knew Kiara had not done that.

Footsteps sounded in the corridor.

Wyatt didn't know why, but he ducked behind the room divider. Guilty conscience most likely.

The door opened.

"It's done," the woman said, and he recognized the voice as Lauren's. Was she talking to him? Had she seen him dive behind the divider?

Feeling sheepish, he was about to come out when he heard her say, "The only thing Decadent Midnight will win now is a vinegar contest."

She must be on the phone.

He thought of the vinegar bottle. Of the syringe in the trash can. A chill of dread moved through him.

"No, thank you, Mr. DeSalme. I can't wait to start working for you."

He almost couldn't believe the implications of what she was saying. He didn't want to believe it, but he knew exactly what his older brothers were capable of. They'd do a lot of underhanded things to win. Like send a corporate spy to monitor their competition. Or get an ambitious intern to spike the competition's superior wine with vinegar.

Rage propelled Wyatt from behind the divider. "What in the hell did you do?"

Lauren shrieked, threw her phone in the air. "Jesus," she cried and splayed a hand over her chest. "You scared the crap out of me."

He stalked toward her. She backpedaled fast. "My brothers put you up to spiking the wine Kiara took to the competition."

Lauren shrugged. "Prove it."

The look on her face was all the proof he needed.

"Your fingerprints are bound to be all over the syringe and bottles."

"Big deal. I could have touched those things at any time. I work in the lab."

"Doesn't matter," he said. "You're not getting away with it."

THE BEST OF the Best Award was being held at the Sonoma Civic Center as part of a four-day-long Fourth of July celebration. The streets were lined with banners welcoming visitors. Tourists packed shops and boutiques. The traffic coming into town moved at a crawl. Kiara had been here before and had expected the delay. It was several hours before they had to have their wine in front of the judges for the taste test, but they had to be registered by noon and it was eleven-fifteen now.

She could feel the tension mounting. What if Decadent Midnight wasn't as good as she thought it was? What if someone like DeSalme blew them out of the water?

They were in DeSalme territory after all. Everywhere they looked signs advertised DeSalme Wineries. People carried shopping bags with the DeSalme Logo etched on them.

What had she been thinking? A tiny family winery didn't stand a chance up against the corporate wines. Those taste tests where consumers went for brand loyalty over taste haunted her.

"Remember Chateau Montelena," Maurice said, reading her mind.

Chateau Montelena was a small winery in Napa Valley that in 1976 beat out a French chardonnay in a blind taste test in France known famously as the

Judgment of Paris and immortalized in the film *Bottle Shock*. The wine had rocked the industry, proving once and for all that California chardonnays could compete with French wines.

"If Chateau Montelena can score against the big boys, we can too."

Kiara glanced over at her cousin. She and Maurice had had their differences. Philosophically, they disagreed on almost everything. But they were family and right now, she felt closer to Maurice than anyone.

"Thanks for holding my hand," she said.

"Hey, you and I clash a lot, but we're both Romanos." Maurice smiled. "Do you remember that time when we were kids and we visited the DeSalme Winery?"

Kiara shook her head. "No."

"You were probably too young. I was around eight, so you would have been what, five?"

"Why were we at DeSalme?"

"That was before they went corporate. Back when Richard DeSalme was still running the place."

"Not ringing a bell." She knew what Maurice was doing, trying to take her mind off the upcoming competition and she appreciated it.

"They invited us to a big cookout, along with several other wine people."

Kiara cast her mind back. "Wait a minute. Did they have a swimming pool and horses?"

"They did."

"Hmm, I do remember it. Vaguely."

"I'm Eric's age. We got into a wrestling match. He beat me, but he cheated, put me in a full Nelson."

"Oh, well, your skills lie elsewhere, cousin."

A memory flitted. She remembered the smell of

barbecue, a group of rowdy children running through vineyards, playing tag. She was "it" and she walked to the end of the row and there had been a boy about her own age, with compelling chocolate-brown eyes. An odd sensation ran through her. Eyes the same color as Wyatt's.

Wyatt.

She felt badly about that. He'd tried to call her several times, but she'd let it go to voice mail. She still wasn't ready to talk to him. Still hadn't sorted out how she was going to deal with these scary feelings. Once this competition was behind her, she'd be ready to sit down with him and have an honest discussion.

Maurice navigated the Civic Center parking lot, and parked in a spot reserved for contestants. Kiara quickly forget the memory as they took four crates from the back and loaded them onto the rolling dolly. She wondered if she'd been fooling herself. The wine was good. But did they honestly stand a chance of taking the Best of the Best against DeSalme?

When they were finished loading, Maurice wheeled the dolly toward the Civic Center and Kiara trotted ahead so she could open the door for them. A blast of cool air hit them as they entered the long corridor leading to the event room where the judging would take place.

The center was a bustle of activity. Contestants, judges and ancillary staff buzzing around, setting up. A news crew was on hand from a local news station. The walls of the corridors were plastered with advertising, most of it from wineries throughout California. Bella Notte hadn't been able to afford the advertising that often ran to six figures.

"I heard DeSalme is unveiling a new advertising campaign today," Maurice said, reading her thoughts again.

"We certainly can't compete with them on that score."

"No worries." Maurice grinned. "We'll let our wine do the talking. After this, word of mouth will be all we need."

"I don't know about that."

"Stop thinking about that taste test you conducted in grad school. It was one test, years ago."

They had almost reached the door where contestants were supposed to enter. There, plastered from floor to ceiling was DeSalme's new poster.

The slogan read DeSalme, from our family to yours.

But that's not what stopped Kiara in her tracks, Maurice kept walking, not noticing that the panoramic poster had ensnared her.

Beneath the slogan was a picture of the DeSalme winery, stretching out, classy and beautiful. To the left side of the poster, superimposed over the vineyards was a picture of the DeSalme brothers.

She'd always thought there were just two DeSalmes, but this picture depicted three siblings, their names emblazed under their photos in elegant script. Scott. Eric. Wyatt.

From the poster, Wyatt's brown eyes met Kiara's. His hair was cut short and he wasn't wearing glasses, but it was Wyatt.

It took her a second to process what she was seeing. Why was Wyatt Jordan's picture on the poster for DeSalme wine?

Did that mean…

Oh, dear God. Her stomach lurched and for one horrible second, she thought she was going to throw up.

The man who'd been working at Bella Notte for the past month, the man she'd just spent the night with on Twin Hearts. The man she'd shared a bottle of Decadent Midnight with under a full moon on the last day of June. The man she'd fallen in love with was up there on the poster with Scott and Eric DeSalme.

The truth hit her with the force of an open-handed slap.

Wyatt was a corporate spy.

12

Blind tasting: To taste wines without knowing their identity.

"KIARA?" MAURICE CALLED her name.

She stood there in a daze, her eyes fixed on Wyatt's charming printed smile.

Maurice followed her gaze. "What the hell?"

The air-conditioning was chilling her to the bone. Slowly, haltingly, she faced her cousin. "Let's go check in," she said, keeping her voice completely emotionless.

"That's Wyatt."

"I see that."

"He's a DeSalme."

"So it seems."

"You didn't know?"

"Did you?"

"No, of course not."

She shook herself. "It's getting late. We need to register."

"What are you going to do about that?" Maurice jerked a thumb at the mural.

"There's nothing to be done. Come on." She squared her shoulders against the desolation battering her heart and walked through the door.

Her cell phone rang. She looked at the caller ID: Wyatt.

Part of her wanted to answer it and scream at him, but the calm scientist in her powered off the phone. No more distractions from him. She was here to win this competition and that's what she intended on doing.

They were given a number and an instruction sheet. They had two hours to kill. This was tortuous.

"Do you want to get something to eat?" Maurice asked.

"I couldn't eat."

Her cousin put a hand on her shoulder. "I'm sorry about Wyatt."

"I'll live."

"I know you liked him."

Loved. She loved him.

You can't love him. You don't even know him. He's a liar. He put on a mask. He showed you the face he wanted you to see. The glasses were probably even fake.

"You want to get drunk?" Maurice asked.

"Tempting as that sounds, it's no cure. Thanks for the offer though. But I would like to taste the wine. Just a reassurance that it is as good as I think it is."

"Okay," Maurice said. He opened a crate, took out a bottle of Decadent Midnight. He gave it to her to hold while he went to find a glass.

Kiara's nose twitched. She smelled vinegar. Who smelled like vinegar? She scanned the growing crowd.

Maurice handed her a glass. She poured an ounce of wine, lifted it to her nose. Vinegar. She blinked, shook her head. Something was wrong. She took a tiny sip. Phew.

"Vinegar." Tears sprang to Kiara's eyes. "It tastes like vinegar."

"How is that possible?" A scowl creased Maurice's forehead.

"Open another bottle."

Maurice twisted out the cork on another one. He took one sniff. "Vinegar."

"Another." She could hear her voice go wire-thin, garroting off her air.

Maurice opened another one, shook his head.

"They've been tampered with," Kiara said with utter despair.

"Wyatt DeSalme." Maurice spat out the name. "He spiked our wine."

Wyatt might have been spying on them, but Kiara did not want to believe he'd stooped to spiking their wine. Could not believe it. Not the man who had so tenderly made love to her underneath the full moon.

Wake up and smell the wine, sister. He screwed you over. In more ways than one.

That pain that shot through her heart was agony. It was a special kind of hell. She'd opened up her home, her winery, her heart to Wyatt and this was how he'd repaid her.

Lies.

Every word he'd spoken had been a lie. The tender lovemaking they'd shared on Twin Hearts, nothing but a lie, a charade, a con. So much for romantic legend. The myth was officially busted. She'd shared a bottle of wine with him under the full moon in June and they were not fated. He was not her destiny. At least not the good kind of destiny. She'd been nothing but a pawn in the DeSalmes' ploy to crush their competition. She was a fool.

"Contestants," came an announcement over the loud speaker. "It's now time to bring your wine to the sommelier at the front of the room. You have fifteen minutes to get your wine turned in so it can be marked for the judging."

"It's over," she told Maurice. "Let's pack up this salad dressing and get the hell back to Idyll."

Maurice stared at her as if she'd sprouted a second head. "I don't believe it."

"What?" She couldn't meet his eyes. Could barely keep breathing. How was it possible to hurt so much and still keep breathing?

She'd fought so hard against falling in love with Wyatt. Had resisted and resisted, but he'd worn her down. Made her believe she could have everything she ever wanted, but had been too afraid to wish for. This was why she'd been so afraid. Terrified of feeling exactly like she was feeling now.

Betrayed.

"You," Maurice said. "Throwing in the towel. Giving up without a fight. It's not like you, Kiara."

"Things have changed."

"You're not the first person to be betrayed by love."

"No, but I'm the first Romano who has been."

Maurice grabbed her by the shoulders. "I won't let you give up. Fight, Kiara. You have to fight."

"What for?"

"For everything Bella Notte stands for. Love, romance, the best damned wine in California."

"It's too late. There's no way to get a fresh bottle of Decadent Midnight here before the judging. It's over."

"Maybe not," Maurice said.

She was too defeated even to hope, sluggishly she said. "How?"

Maurice nodded toward the exit.

Kiara turned.

The minute she saw him, her heart skipped a beat.

It was Wyatt and he had two bottles of Decadent Midnight in his hands.

A million emotions bombarded her—hurt, sadness, regret, betrayal, foolishness, hope. Stupid hope that somehow there had been a mistake. But he'd probably just come here to gloat. She tightened her jaw, fisted her hands, hardened her heart.

WYATT SAW THE hatred in Kiara's eyes. Felt it like a blow. When he'd seen the advertising on the wall he'd known she'd have figured out who he was. And now that he saw her standing there with Maurice, surrounded by open bottles of Decadent Midnight, he knew she'd also found out that her wine tasted like vinegar.

She stalked toward him, her body trembling with fury. "You bastard!"

Heads turned. A murmur ran through the crowd.

On the drive up, he'd convinced himself he could talk some sense into her, but one look at her face and all hope disappeared.

Kiara was lost to him as surely as if he'd been the one to spike her wine.

"I have fresh bottles," he said by way of an apology. "Get them to the sommelier now."

"How do I know those aren't vinegar too?" She glowered.

"I guess you'll just have to trust me on this."

"I'll take them," Maurice said.

Wyatt handed the bottles to Maurice without even looking away from Kiara. "We have to talk."

"I have nothing to say to you Wyatt *DeSalme*."

"It's true," he said. "I am a DeSalme."

"I don't want to hear it." She began to walk away.

"No!" he said, raising his voice to be heard above the hum of the crowd. "I'm not going to let you put up that wall. I know you want to. You like hiding out. But I'm not going to let you eject me from your life without first hearing me out."

People were really staring now, but he didn't care.

Wyatt held out his hand. "Kiara, come with me."

For the longest time he thought she was not going to respond. Then finally, she turned back, gave a curt nod but wouldn't take his hand. "There's a flower garden across the street from the center," she said. "We can talk there. You have five minutes. That's all the time I'm going to waste on you."

She left by the side exit and Wyatt hurried to catch up with her. Across the street she began to pace around the pink geraniums. The bright, optimistic garden was in harsh contrast to his dark, hopeless mood.

"That wine I brought you is not spiked," he said.

"Had an attack of conscience, did you?"

"I didn't spike it."

She eyed him suspiciously. "Who did?"

"Your intern, Lauren."

"Now why would she do that?"

"Because my brothers paid her to do it."

"Why didn't they pay you to do it?"

"Because I quit being their spy when I realized I was falling in love with you."

Kiara inhaled audibly. "Don't even try to lie to me."

"It's true." He gentled his voice. He could see she was hurting, knew he was the cause of her pain and that ripped him up inside. "I tried to call you and tell you but you wouldn't answer your phone. I left you, like, five hundred voice mails."

"But you've been spying on Bella Notte for a month."

"Guilty," he said. "I didn't know how to break it to you. I didn't want to hurt you."

"Well, you did."

"I know and I'm so, so sorry." He came toward her, hand extended.

She held up a palm. "Stop."

He froze, too far away to touch her but close enough to see the anguish etched into her face.

"I planned to tell you who I was this morning when we woke up," Wyatt said. "Actually, I meant to tell you last night, but well, things kind of got out of hand on that score."

"That's easy enough to say now, in hindsight."

He was trying to smile, but his old standby wasn't working. He gave up the struggle, looked at her beseechingly. "You ran out on me. Why did you run out on me?"

"Oh, no," she said. "You don't get to do this. You don't get to turn this around and make this my fault."

"That's not what I'm trying to do." He rubbed the nape of his neck with a palm. "I'm just trying to explain."

"You're the one who lied. You're the one who spied."

"I'm sorry," he said. "I'm making a mess out of this. And it's the most important speech of my life."

It was the most important speech of her life too. Kiara tightened her arms across her chest, steeling her mind against him, but even as she did it, a part of her was crying out, *listen, listen, maybe he can make this all right.* She longed for him to make it right. She wished she could go back in time and erase everything. Stay by his side, wake up next to him and turn into his embrace instead of running away from the love she was feeling, have things play out the way he'd intended. Let him confess underneath the olive tree instead of here, in front of everyone.

But she hadn't done that and she'd discovered the hard way who he was and…and…*he'd broken her heart.*

This was what she'd feared all along. This was why she'd avoided romantic entanglements. Not because she didn't believe in the family legend, but because secretly, she believed so deeply that she knew that once she fell in love it would be for keeps.

Until Wyatt, no one had ever pushed her out of her comfort zone. No man had ever challenged her the way he did. No one had ever been worth climbing to the top of Twin Hearts for. But she'd done it with him. Made the climb, taken the plunge, drunk the wine and put her heart on the line.

And it had all turned to dust in her hand.

"When I woke up and put together what had happened, that you'd gone to Sonoma without me…" His voice cracked with emotion and he trailed off, his eyes burning into hers. "It just about killed me."

"You think it was easy for me?" she whispered.

The bleak expression, desolate as forsaken land, carved his handsome features. "I was so afraid, Kiara, so scared that you didn't feel for me the same way I felt for you. I tried to tell myself I was keeping this light. No strings attached. That it was just good fun, but I've been lying to myself for weeks now, unable to face the truth."

In Kiara's mind the big, open area narrowed to just the two of them. The tourists, the flowers, vanished. "What truth?"

His hand trembled as he reached for her, closed quivering fingers around her wrist, and stared deeply into her eyes. "That I love you and no amount of pretending otherwise can change it."

He loved her.

She was overcome with emotion; her thoughts whirled; feelings assailed her—fear, hope, excitement. Could it be true? For weeks now she'd been telling herself this was nothing more than lust. She'd warned herself not to get involved. Had done her best to avoid getting serious. But it hadn't worked and now here was Wyatt professing his love for her.

All promises to the contrary, *he* hadn't kept it light either. He was in as deep as she.

The implications washed over her, vast and forceful as a tidal wave. He loved her and she loved him.

"Kiara," he whispered.

Anxiety tinged his voice. Or maybe it was something else. What did she know about him really? He wasn't Wyatt Jordan, charming cork dork, but corporate playboy Wyatt DeSalme. How could she love him when she didn't even know who he was?

Unable to speak, she turned and looked away.

He moved his hand from her wrist to her chin, tilted her face to meet his gaze. "Talk to me, Kiara."

"Who are you?"

"You know me. You know me better than anyone."

"No." She shook her head. "You've been putting on an act, playing a part. You seduced me to get information about my winery. You used me."

"Yes," he said, not denying it. "In the beginning, that's true. But once I met you, once I understood how much Bella Notte meant to you, I stopped spying for my brothers."

"Then why didn't you just leave?" She felt a tearing in the center of her chest.

"Because I wanted to be around you. I needed to be around you."

"You actually expect me to believe that?"

"I stopped talking to my brothers. It's why they approached Lauren to sabotage your wine. They knew my allegiance had changed."

"You're telling me you're not part of DeSalme Wines?"

"I was never really a part of the company. I didn't enjoy the corporate culture. And because of the trust fund my grandmother left me, I'm afraid I was just... irresponsible. But all that changed when I came to Idyll. When I met you."

"So why did you do it? Why did you play spy for your brothers if you weren't a part of DeSalme Wines?"

"I was flattered that they asked for my help. They'd never asked for my help before, and even though I didn't consciously know it, I was looking for where I really belonged."

"Belonged?" she echoed.

"I was tired of playing. Tired of casual affairs. I wanted a solid life, solid work. And I found it. At Bella Notte, with you. I want to make wine the way you make wine. Small-scale, focus on quality, not quantity. Surrounded by family, not suits and spreadsheets. I want an intimate and romantic atmosphere, instead of cold and sterile corporate headquarters. But most of all, Kiara, I want to be with you. Please tell me there's a chance for us."

She stood there looking at the man she'd come to love in a very short length of time. The maelstrom of emotion had vanished, passed through her, quieted. In the lemon tree a blue jay scolded.

Slowly, she held out her hand to Wyatt.

He didn't bother taking her hand, but instead let loose with a whoop of joy and pulled her into his arms. "Kiara." He covered her face in kisses.

"We've still got a way to go."

"I know. I'll be patient. I'll prove myself to you. I'll tell you everything about me."

She nodded. "I'm sorry for running out on you this morning. That wasn't a very mature thing to do."

"I understood."

"You've got a big heart, Wyatt."

He reached up to wipe away the tear she hadn't even known had tracked down her cheek. "Not as big as yours, Kiara Romano. So as far as the legend goes, is that myth just a myth or confirmed?"

She couldn't help but smile. "That myth's confirmed."

He put his arm around her shoulder. "C'mon. Let's go watch Decadent Midnight kick DeSalmes' ass."

Epilogue

*Grafting: The act of attaching one plant to
another so that the two will grow into one.*

DECADENT MIDNIGHT DID indeed take first place in the
Best of the Best. And Wyatt insisted his brothers pay
restitution for the Bella Notte wine they'd spoiled. In
typical form, they refused to give him the job they'd
promised and even took his face off the advertising,
but they did apologize to Kiara for the vinegar incident.

Wyatt didn't care about not working for his brothers. He'd found his true home. On Idyll, at Bella Notte,
with Kiara and her warm, welcoming family.

The following June, under a full moon, they got married at the top of Twin Hearts, adding another perfect
romance to the legend of Idyll Island. Their families and
friends came. Even Scott and Eric, who were on their
best behavior. Steve showed up as well. He'd turned out
to have a talent for knowing the exact right moment to
pick late-harvest grapes, so he stayed on at Bella Notte.
Lauren did indeed go to work at DeSalme. She and
Eric were dating and quite often, she put him in a full
Nelson.

Wyatt, with his charming ways and unexpected head for business, finagled a proper distribution agreement for Decadent Midnight that increased Bella Notte's revenue tenfold. Allowing more money for research and development. Kiara's dad remained cancer-free and he and Kiara's mother were planning an Alaskan cruise.

Kiara and Wyatt were spending their honeymoon on Idyll. Neither one of them wanted to stray far from the vineyard they both loved. After the wedding guests had departed, Kiara took her husband by the hand and led him to their spot beneath the olive tree.

"You know," he said. "Whenever I think back on my days growing up on my family vineyard I get this flash of playing tag in the vineyards and this little red-haired girl looking so stern and serious and tagging me out."

"That was me. Your family invited mine to a barbecue. I have flashes of a little brown-eyed boy plowing into me."

Wyatt's smile split his face. "I should have known that was you."

"I hope he looks just like you did when he's five. Gap-toothed, brown eyes, cute little flop of hair over his forehead."

Wyatt frowned. What was she talking about? "He who?"

Kiara put a hand to her belly. "Okay, it might be a she, but I still hope she gets your eyes."

It took a moment for the words to register. "You're pregnant?"

Kiara nodded happily. "Six weeks."

"That's why you wouldn't drink any wine at the wedding."

She ducked her head. "That's it."

Excitement sent his pulse throbbing. "I'm going to be a dad?"

"You are," she confirmed.

It was an earth-shattering moment for a man who'd once thought he wasn't the kind to ever settle down. A dad. He was going to be a dad.

"Are you happy?" she asked. "You can be honest. I won't be upset if you're not overjoyed. I understand this is a lot—"

"Kiara." Her name came out on a husky breath of air and Wyatt reached for her, pulling her into his embrace. He kissed her. "I'm happy." He kissed her again. "I'm excited." Another kiss, harder this time. "I'm thrilled at the notion of being a father."

He felt her relax in his arms. She'd been worried. He kissed her again for good measure, squeezed her tightly. "I can't think of better news."

"It's not going to crimp your style?"

"Sweetheart," Wyatt said, "crimp away. I love the kinks and twists that I've experienced ever since I came to Idyll. You have turned me every which way but loose and I am so grateful for that. For you." He paused and placed a hand to her belly. "And now for our baby."

"Wine will be in his blood."

"Can't avoid that," Wyatt said. "She'll be growing up in a winery."

"Surrounded by his family."

"Who love her very much."

"You really want a girl?"

"One who looks just like you." Wyatt pressed his lips to her throat. She tasted of salty sea air. His Kiara.

"I want a boy who looks just like you."

"We could have twins," he said hopefully.

"I think we should take them one baby at a time."

"C'mon," he said and laid her down on the blanket.

Then as the full moon rose over Idyll and sleepy stars dotted the sky, Kiara and Wyatt made love slowly and sweetly, far into the decadent midnight.

* * * * *

PASSION

For a spicier, decidedly hotter read—
these are your destination for romances!

COMING NEXT MONTH
AVAILABLE NOVEMBER 22, 2011

#651 MERRY CHRISTMAS, BABY
Vicki Lewis Thompson,
Jennifer LaBrecque,
Rhonda Nelson

#652 RED-HOT SANTA
Uniformly Hot!
Tori Carrington

#653 THE MIGHTY QUINNS: KELLAN
The Mighty Quinns
Kate Hoffmann

#654 IT HAPPENED ONE CHRISTMAS
The Wrong Bed
Leslie Kelly

#655 SEXY SILENT NIGHTS
Forbidden Fantasies
Cara Summers

#656 SEX, LIES, AND MISTLETOE
Undercover Operatives
Tawny Weber

You can find more information on upcoming Harlequin® titles,
free excerpts and more at www.HarlequinInsideRomance.com.

REQUEST YOUR FREE BOOKS!
2 FREE NOVELS PLUS 2 FREE GIFTS!

red-hot reads!

YES! Please send me 2 FREE Harlequin® Blaze™ novels and my 2 FREE gifts (gifts are worth about $10). After receiving them, if I don't wish to receive any more books, I can return the shipping statement marked "cancel." If I don't cancel, I will receive 6 brand-new novels every month and be billed just $4.49 per book in the U.S. or $4.96 per book in Canada. That's a saving of at least 14% off the cover price. It's quite a bargain. Shipping and handling is just 50¢ per book in the U.S. and 75¢ per book in Canada.* I understand that accepting the 2 free books and gifts places me under no obligation to buy anything. I can always return a shipment and cancel at any time. Even if I never buy another book, the two free books and gifts are mine to keep forever.

151/351 HDN FEQE

Name _____ (PLEASE PRINT)

Address _____ Apt. #

City _____ State/Prov. _____ Zip/Postal Code

Signature (if under 18, a parent or guardian must sign)

Mail to the Reader Service:
IN U.S.A.: P.O. Box 1867, Buffalo, NY 14240-1867
IN CANADA: P.O. Box 609, Fort Erie, Ontario L2A 5X3

Not valid for current subscribers to Harlequin Blaze books.

**Want to try two free books from another line?
Call 1-800-873-8635 or visit www.ReaderService.com.**

* Terms and prices subject to change without notice. Prices do not include applicable taxes. Sales tax applicable in N.Y. Canadian residents will be charged applicable taxes. Offer not valid in Quebec. This offer is limited to one order per household. All orders subject to credit approval. Credit or debit balances in a customer's account(s) may be offset by any other outstanding balance owed by or to the customer. Please allow 4 to 6 weeks for delivery. Offer available while quantities last.

Your Privacy—The Reader Service is committed to protecting your privacy. Our Privacy Policy is available online at www.ReaderService.com or upon request from the Reader Service.

We make a portion of our mailing list available to reputable third parties that offer products we believe may interest you. If you prefer that we not exchange your name with third parties, or if you wish to clarify or modify your communication preferences, please visit us at www.ReaderService.com/consumerschoice or write to us at Reader Service Preference Service, P.O. Box 9062, Buffalo, NY 14269. Include your complete name and address.

Lucy Flemming and Ross Mitchell shared a magical,
sexy Christmas weekend together six years ago.
This Christmas, history may repeat itself when they find
themselves stranded in a major snowstorm...
and alone at last.

Read on for a sneak peek from
IT HAPPENED ONE CHRISTMAS
by Leslie Kelly.

Available December 2011, only from Harlequin® Blaze™.

EYEING THE GRAY, THICK SKY through the expansive wall of windows, Lucy began to pack up her photography gear. The Christmas party was winding down, only a dozen or so people remaining on this floor, which had been transformed from cubicles and meeting rooms to a holiday funland. She smiled at those nearest to her, then, seeing the glances at her silly elf hat, she reached up to tug it off her head.

Before she could do it, however, she heard a voice. A deep, male voice—smooth and sexy, and so not Santa's.

"I appreciate you filling in on such short notice. I've heard you do a terrific job."

Lucy didn't turn around, letting her brain process what she was hearing. Her whole body had stiffened, the hairs on the back of her neck standing up, her skin tightening into tiny goose bumps. Because that voice sounded so familiar. *Impossibly* familiar.

It can't be.

"It sounds like the kids had a great time."

Unable to stop herself, Lucy began to turn around, wondering if her ears—and all her other senses—were deceiving her. After all, six years was a long time, the mind could play tricks. What were the odds that she'd bump into *him,* here? And today of all days. December 23.

Six years exactly. Was that really possible?

One look—and the accompanying frantic thudding of her heart—and she knew her ears and brain were working just fine. Because it was *him.*

"Oh, my God," he whispered, shocked, frozen, staring as thoroughly as she was. "Lucy?"

She nodded slowly, not taking her eyes off him, wondering why the years had made him even more attractive than ever. It didn't seem fair. Not when she'd spent the past six years thinking he must have started losing that thick, golden-brown hair, or added a spare tire to that trim, muscular form.

No.

The man was gorgeous. Truly, without-a-doubt, mouth-wateringly handsome, every bit as hot as he'd been the first time she'd laid eyes on him. She'd been twenty-two, he one year older.

They'd shared an amazing holiday season.

And had never seen one another again.

Until now.

Find out what happens in
IT HAPPENED ONE CHRISTMAS
by Leslie Kelly.
Available December 2011, only from Harlequin® Blaze™

HBEXP1211

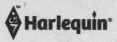